Jenny Eclair is the *Sunday Times* author of four critically acclaimed novels: *Camberwell Beauty*; *Having a Lovely Time*; *Life, Death and Vanilla Slices* and *Moving*. One of the UK's most popular writer/performers, she was the first woman to win the prestigious Perrier Award and has many TV and radio credits to her name. She lives in South-East London.

By Jenny Eclair

Camberwell Beauty
Having a Lovely Time
Life, Death and Vanilla Slices
Moving
Listening In

Listening In

Stories

Jenny Eclair

with illustrations by the author

SPHERE

First published in Great Britain in 2017 by Sphere
This paperback edition published in 2019 by Sphere

1 3 5 7 9 10 8 6 4 2

A CIP catalogue record for this book is available from the British Library.

ISBN 978-0-7515-6707-6

Typeset in Goudy by M Rules
Printed and bound in Great Britain by Clays Ltd, Elcograf S.p.A.

Papers used by Sphere are from well-managed forests
and other responsible sources.

Sphere
An imprint of
Little, Brown Book Group
Carmelite House
50 Victoria Embankment
London EC4Y 0DZ

An Hachette UK Company
www.hachette.co.uk

www.littlebrown.co.uk

For all the women and all their stories

Contents

1	Margot's Cardigans	1
2	A Slight Alteration	11
3	Fantastic News	21
4	Beverley in Shoes	31
5	Christine Paints	41
6	A Trolley for a Change	51
7	First Impressions	61
8	Bones	75
9	Anthea's Round Robin	85
10	Fifteen Minutes to Landing	95
11	Mothers and Daughters	105
12	Valerie Lashes Out	115
13	Lorna's Holiday	125
14	George's Cake	135
15	Holiday Letdown	145
16	Carol Goes Swimming	155
17	Waiting for Billy	165
18	Leo's Passport	175

19	Doing the Best for Daniel	185
20	The Viewing	195
21	Sitting	205
22	The Understudy	217
23	Hannah's Gone	227
24	Points	237

Acknowledgements

Massive thanks to Radio 4 for first approaching me to write some fifteen-minute short stories/monologues, and to Sally Avens for producing them.

To my editor, Antonia Hodgson, for suggesting we create a collection and allowing me to play illustrator, and to Geof and Phoebe for trying not to laugh at some of my drawings.

Margot's Cardigans

I caught sight of her at the back of the charity shop. She was always a dressy woman and I recognised the coat: cream mohair, leopard-skin collar and big fancy resin buttons with what looked like jet-black beetles trapped inside. I felt myself go a bit dizzy, like I used to feel before the doctor diagnosed me with high blood pressure and put me on the pills. I'd not seen Margot Houghton in years.

Only it wasn't Margot Houghton, it was a plastic mannequin, bald as a coot, dressed up in Margot Houghton's clothes, with Margot Houghton's black patent handbag dangling from what looked like an oddly dislocated arm, as if Margot Houghton might have recently fallen off a bus.

I'd only gone in to look at a piece of Royal Worcester; I've been collecting china birds since I first got married. My sister

Maeve got me started, she bought Bill and me two porcelain chaffinches perched on a stump of wood for a wedding present, stamped and everything. After that I was hooked. Don't get me wrong, I'm not china-bird bonkers, I'm selective, although I did branch out into plates a few years ago and now I've got a whole wall of them, but I don't buy fakes and I don't buy chipped. It's good to have a hobby – takes your mind off all the other crap.

Very nearly fifty years married, me and Bill. People were surprised when we got together because I was a bit of a live wire and he was a sensible man, very quiet.

I turned myself down a few notches for Bill. I knew he was a safe bet, steady with his drink, good driver, bit boring if I'm honest, but I didn't want to live like my mum, I didn't want Friday-night fights and black eyes and sending the kids round to Auntie Marion's to get us out the way and keep us fed.

I wanted safe and I didn't want any surprises, and yes, sometimes I could have screamed at Bill, the way he ate his boiled eggs, and his cod-liver breath, but I swallowed it all back and I kept a nice tidy house and we had one nice tidy kid who was never any trouble and still visits every other Sunday, even though he lives in Macclesfield and his wife is a bitch.

My sister used to come to the shops with me, but she died last year. I miss her and I think about the old days a lot, but I make sure I don't just sit indoors and get morbid.

Let's face it, there's only so much daytime telly you can stand before you start yelling and telling the lot of them to

'Shut your silly cakehole', and that includes the big chap off *Pointless*.

Drives me mad, all them clever fellas, think they know everything. It's only facts. I don't think women care about facts, we care about the other stuff, the stuff that gets you through life: how to make a decent roast potato, which jar of pickled onions give the best crunch, how to get a grape out of a toddler's throat when it's choking.

I might not have any qualifications to speak of but I've got common sense coming out of my ears and eyes in the back of my head.

Which is why, twenty years ago, I didn't trust Margot Houghton as far as I could throw her – because that's another thing us women have: instinct. Instinct and imagination, we can put two and two together and see disaster.

Bill never had either. He'd never look out of the window and take a guess at the weather, he'd never sniff the air and reckon it might rain, he would give the barometer a polite knock instead. He relied on instruments, on science and experts.

I'm not like that, I get a feeling in my water and shivers down my spine; hairs prickle on the back of my neck, and sometimes I get a metallic taste at the back of my tongue.

I can always tell which way the wind is blowing. I'm like a rabbit – you know how they sit up and twitch, every nerve ending on guard? Well, I'm like that.

I've got a nose for trouble, comes from being brought up in a house where you could smell a bad mood before it came round the door and gave you a crack on the side of the head.

I learnt to creep around when I was a kid, knew how to keep myself small so as not to be seen. I just hung back, listening and watching.

I notice things. Bill never noticed anything, unless I went mad and put a pair of red socks in his underwear drawer. 'Oh no, Ivy, not red' – he liked his socks plain navy, didn't have an ounce of flash in him. 'Got to watch the quiet ones', that's what my sister Maeve said, then she married a chap by the name of Neville Brewster. He could have talked the hind legs off donkeys for a living. Ended up doing a stretch for tax evasion; she said it was quite nice having the house to herself.

I like ornaments, maybe because we never had any when I was growing up. Anything my mum liked, he'd have broken, and she'd have to glue it back together. I can't be doing with big seams of lumpy glue. Once something's broken, it's broken. It might as well be smashed to smithereens as have a tiny little crack in it.

I do the car boots and the charity shops and there's plenty of them where I live. Ageing population, you see, not much what they call disposable income. We like a bargain, us old biddies. There's hundreds of us round here, swarming around, sniffing for bargains.

Sometimes I buy the odd blouse or skirt, but really I'm on the lookout for china birds.

'You can just get them off the internet, Mum', that's what my son tells me. He got me an iPad and showed me how to do eBay, but it's too easy, there's not the thrill of the chase. I believe in things finding you as much as you finding them, so I just keep my eyes open and sometimes . . . Bingo.

Today it was a kingfisher in the window of Cancer Research with a fish in its beak, price tag turned the wrong way round. They do that on purpose.

The trick is not to go in too keen. You've got to look like you're not that fussed, don't make a beeline for anything.

And then I saw pretend Margot and I watched myself go the colour of bleached linen in the shop mirror.

One of the lady volunteers – you know the type, never done a day's proper work, still all at sea with the till – noticed me gawping at the mannequin. 'Very swish, isn't it, that coat? Lovely donation.'

'We got a job lot of cardigans too,' adds her fat little volunteer friend.

'Cashmere,' they chorused.

'In every colour.'

'We've put a few out, but we're saving some back.'

'We don't want a mad rush.'

They seemed to be taking it in turns to speak.

I wandered over to the knitwear rail and starting rummaging along the coat hangers. There was a pale pink cardigan, colour of a baby's toenail, and I checked the label: 100 per cent cashmere. The one next to it was a deep plum colour, they wanted fifteen pounds for it and I couldn't decide whether to choose the plum or go for a deep moss-green one with gilt buttons.

'We've shoes too,' said Tweedledee.

'Very nice quality,' said Tweedledum.

'But she was a size six,' I said, 'and I'm a five.'

'That's right,' they choroused.

They weren't listening to me. One of them started ferreting under the desk. 'And some costume jewellery.' She puffed and brought up a tray of bits, brooches and earrings, nothing decent, just some beads, a bit of paste.

'House clearance?' I asked.

And off they went again: 'Not exactly.'

'Her son brought this lot in.'

'She's gone into the Hazelmere.'

'He's selling the house.'

'Doesn't live round here.'

I bought the plum cardi. I knew it would be a bit tight, she was a twelve, was Margot, slimmer than me and much taller. I didn't bother with the kingfisher, then I caught the bus up to the Hazelmere.

Matron was most accommodating: as long as I signed the visitors' book I was welcome to pop up and see Margot. Honestly, I could have been Harold Shipman in drag.

She was in a small room round the back of the nursing home. I knew the drill, I've visited other friends in this place – not that Margot is a friend, of course, but even so. I sat in the chair by the bed as she slept and breathed so quietly that I couldn't be quite sure ... although she was alive because her nightie moved a tiny fraction every couple of seconds, and we chatted.

Or rather, I chatted. I told her about the weather outside and how I'd seen a kingfisher this morning and for a bit I pretended it was a real one, then I confessed it was made of china and stuck in the window of the charity shop, and I told her how I knew her son was packing up the bungalow and I asked her how she felt about being dumped in a home and said how I thought my son would have the decency to invite me to see my days out at his house, even though his wife might not like it.

Nothing, she didn't even flinch, and I knew then that she wasn't going to wake up, so I carried on chatting about this and that while I went through her locker.

Everyone has a locker in a nursing home, a locker and a wardrobe, like a geriatrics' boarding school, and I found the leather box very easily. No one had thought to disguise it or even hide it, it was just sitting there. Inside were her wedding and engagement rings, a double strand of pearls with matching drop earrings and a nice gold bracelet, simple but twenty-four carat, inlaid with alternate diamond and ruby chips.

It went over my wrist quite easily and I pushed it under my sleeve so that I could give Matron a cheery goodbye without drawing attention to the thing, and then I waited for a bus that would take me home.

I thought about getting off early and nipping into the fish shop to get some salmon fillet for supper but then I remembered how much I'd paid for the cardigan. Anyway, I've plenty squirrelled away in the freezer and Bill's not fussy.

He's a very undemanding man, Bill. Never been any trouble, apart from that one time.

I watched it happen with my own eyes, the first time they were having a coffee together right next to Bill's accountancy office and I gave them the benefit of the doubt. It was business; Bill was being typically kind to that poor widow woman, Margot whatserface, the one whose husband dropped down dead at the Winter Gardens.

But then suddenly she was everywhere, buying a new hat in Stringers, in the library changing her historical romances, dancing with Bill at the golf club annual fundraiser. Then I saw him with her at Ken and Glenda Fellowes's bonfire party. I watched him stroke her arm and just for a second I saw them hold hands. It was so quick I wasn't sure if I'd imagined it, but then I saw him in Redfern's the jewellers just before Christmas and I thought, What are you doing in there, you silly fool? I stood on the pavement, my feet like frozen turnips and I watched the assistant take a gold bracelet out of the window and he never put it back, and then Bill walked out with a stupid look on his face and in that split-second I knew.

I knew it wasn't my Christmas present: he'd already given me the money for a tumble drier.

I could have turned into my dad, I could have drunk every bottle on our drinks table in the dining room and set about smashing everything up. I could have put my fist through his stupid barometer and pissed in his shoes.

But I didn't. I made a resolution and I sat it out. I was extra nice to him and made him Scotch eggs of a weekend; I kept the house immaculate and always let him have the first bath. I gave him seconds of custard and dripped stories into his ear about expensive divorces and kids gone wrong from broken homes and I banged on about how well our son was doing, what with him coming from a stable, supportive background and not having anything to worry about while he sat his exams.

I became more willing in bed. I tried harder – not that he was the adventurous type, but I was extra loving, complimented him more, met him for lunch at the office. I made it impossible for him to slip away: I would always offer to go with him or give him a lift, I was like a shadow to that man, and eventually they must have run out of steam because she simply disappeared off the scene.

Apparently she went to live with her cousin in Spain. Rumour had it the climate suited her and she only came home a couple of times a year.

After supper (pork chops with a marmalade glaze), Bill and I sit on the sofa together and watch television. We have the subtitles on because neither of us hears very well, and occasionally he will hold my hand.

We are not a particularly demonstrative couple – we don't go in for cuddling – but we are affectionate and tonight Bill strokes the sleeve of my cardigan as if I were some kind of pet that he is very fond of, and as his fingers touch the gold bracelet he lifts my wrist to his tortoiseshell glasses for closer inspection. He looks puzzled and asks 'Is this new?' and I say, 'Yes darling, it's my fiftieth wedding anniversary present from you.'

Then I go and get my husband and myself a mini Magnum from the freezer to celebrate. Almond for me, vanilla for Bill.

In a minute he might notice the bracelet again and ask me the same question, 'Is this new?'

I could answer him anything; he won't remember. My husband fell off a ladder five years ago redecorating the ceiling in the spare room. His balance has gone and his short-term memory has been badly affected. I still love him, but there's a crack in his brain and no amount of glue can make him perfect again. I can tell him anything I like, he won't remember. I don't even think he remembers Margot Houghton, but I do.

2

A Slight Alteration

I tell you, I've had it with this material. Some kind of taffeta, slippery and stiff, yards of the stuff. I'm taking the hem up by hand – I've been at it forever. I feel like I'm stitching round the moon.

She came in a few weeks ago, one of those breathy in-a-hurry, on-her-way-to-somewhere-else girls. Says her name is Imogen and can I sort this frock out?

It used to be her great-auntie's: fifties, good quality, Bond Street label, very dark green with a purple sheen like a dragonfly. She wants it to fit like a glove. I don't know why people say that; you can't wear a glove.

I've always been good with a needle, right from when I was a kid in primary. Cross-stitch we did first of all, silky embroidery thread, little stitches in and out, then my nana give me a go on her old Singer and I soon got to grips with that, so I got a second-hand one for Christmas and I was off.

To be honest, I never wanted to do it full time, it was just a hobby. You get ever such a hunch if you sew all day every day, end up all bent over like a banana.

I used to make my Sally little summer frocks for when we went on holiday, and fancy-dress costumes: she won ever such a lot of first prizes. Of course nowadays it's big business is fancy dress, and you can buy all sorts of things off the internet. I saw something the other day, little kiddie dressed up as a bowl of meatballs on noodles. You can't make that sort of thing at home.

I used to work in the building society but a load of us counter staff got made redundant because people would rather do their banking online and who can blame them? Which would you rather do, spend your Friday lunchtime in Pizza Express or stand on your bunions in a queue?

So I set up a little sideline doing bespoke upholstery and alterations.

The middle classes like their things handmade, they like the idea of a little woman in Nunhead who runs up their Liberty-print fabrics.

I'm the little treasure that re-covers that sofa the kids have been eating their dinner off for years and makes it look like new. I've a lady in Camberwell, calls me 'the transformer'. I don't need to advertise, it's all word of mouth and now I've got premises. I rent a space in a dry-cleaner's – its useful for the big stuff, I've an industrial machine and because I'm in the window I get a lot of passing trade. Mostly alterations: some people literally can't sew a button on. My daughter's like that. I wish she'd learn, it's good to be able to take your mind off yourself, might keep her hands out the biscuit tin. She could do with a job. I said to her, you'll turn into that sofa one day.

I get lost in fabric. Bit of radio on in the background and before I know it another day's done.

Apparently I come highly recommended. This Imogen's mum knows someone in Highshore Road who I did some 'smashing roman blinds' for.

Apart from shortening this dress, I've to let it out at the bust and take it in at the waist. We did a proper measure last week, she popped in after the gym, five foot three, nine stone give or take, curvy yet petite. A pocket Venus, isn't that the phrase? Her skin is creamy and unmarked, save for a small brown mole on the blade of her shoulder. Her stomach gurgled as I put the measure around her waist, twenty-five inches. 'I should be able to get that down to twenty-four inches,' she says, 'I'm only eating low-cal hummus and carrots, and I'm going to the gym three times a week.' But then her mobile phone goes off and she agrees to meet someone called Cam for a pint at the Queens. 'Flatmate,' she grinned, but not for much longer, and she twisted a diamond solitaire around her little-girl finger. That's another thing I've noticed: some women never grow adult hands. I have, mine are capable, they have to be. I've put up with a lot.

I'm sixty, I've buried both my parents (not personally), been divorced, made redundant. There's a lot of stuff goes round in my head, a lot of 'what ifs', and I'm glad the sewing machine drowns it all out, sat there on the table blocking out the light like a great big mechanical cat, jabber-jabber, its needle-sharp teeth biting into the fabric.

I made my daughter's wedding dress. She was a size fourteen when we started looking at patterns and a size twelve when I sewed on the last seed pearl. I've never seen her so lovely.

'Don't go losing too much weight,' I said to Imogen. 'You're just right as you are.'

'That's what my fiancé says,' she giggled, and we agreed she'd come in the following week after her gym session and bring in the heels she wanted to wear with the dress.

'It's for my engagement party,' she tells me. 'I'm going to have my hair done all fifties-style.' She's got lovely hair, auburn and thick. She wanted to show me a photo of her auntie, swiped through her phone until she found one. Like a proper old-fashioned pin-up, this Eileen woman – imagine Princess Margaret, but even more of a goer – and as she handed me the phone for a closer look I accidentally swiped the screen and I saw him . . .

Cottage cheese and oranges, that's all my Sall ate for months. Swimming, jogging, yoga – she said she had to be perfect for Nick. She had him on a pedestal; that was the problem. Don't get me wrong, he was a catch: worked in corporate finance, dishy too. Our Sally hit the jackpot with Mr N. Bradmore, younger son of the Bradmores of Wandsworth Common, four-bedroom semi, gravel drive, off-street parking for his and hers Mercedes.

His parents weren't mad on me, I was still at the building society back then. His mum didn't work, she told me she was a 'stay-at-home mummy to my two darling boys'. Well, Nick was twenty-eight and his brother was even older, silly cow. I think they were surprised by me, I think Sall had led them to imagine something a bit more classy. She made me park my car three streets away and she talked to Nick and his family in a completely different voice and laughed like she'd been practising a new laugh.

They never came to mine. Don't get me wrong, my soft furnishings are top-notch, but it don't matter how fancy your loose covers are, it's still a two-bedroom ex-local authority on the Dog Kennel Hill estate. Sally's always wanted more, always been a bit jealous. I think it comes from being fat as a kid and being bullied, it was like she had something to prove and Nick was the key to the life she wanted. It wasn't like her dad was going to help out. First thing he did after leaving me was fall under a bus, useless lump.

I should have seen it coming, I've got eyes like a blimming hawk – I've unpicked seams that look perfectly straight to anyone else. I should have seen things had gone wonky and I'm not talking about sofa cushions here, I'm talking about real life.

She's very chatty is Imogen, bubbly, she's a PA for the directors of a global finance company. That's where she met her fiancé and her face glows. Stinks of happiness, does Imogen.

They've hired the function room of a bowls club, she says, it's all going to be retro, even the food, and they've got a swing band. She says her fiancé thinks she's a bit potty but he just wants her to be happy. The shoes are vintage too,

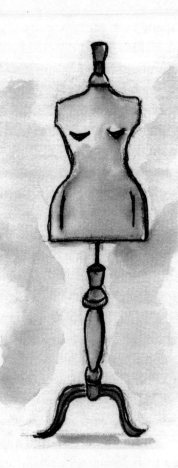

dove-grey suede with a bit of a platform. She's got good ankles and I pin the dress to bang on the knee, and she starts giggling and says, 'Of course, Nick likes the idea of me wearing suspenders too.' She keeps laughing; a pin pierces my skin and blood bubbles up like a ladybird on the tip of my finger.

'Occupational hazard,' I say, but my head pounds and I feel sick. I've never been good with blood.

The dress is a tiny bit tight on the waist but she says she can drop at least two pounds if she sticks to miso soup and we arrange for her to pick up the dress next Thursday, after her gym session. I remind her I close at seven. I've got my own life to get back to.

Though some nights I'm tempted to stay here, curled up in the back room. Make myself a nest of scraps, let the fumes from the dry-cleaning solution knock me out.

I could put the radio on, but I don't, I sit in silence sewing this endless hem and I can't help going over old ground and feeling angry, because I liked him very much, and I was relieved because I thought, at last, someone else is going to be responsible for her happiness. I tell you, having kids is easy, but loving them is knackering.

My daughter's wedding dress hung on the door of her old bedroom. Her last night spent in her little single bed. Late at night she knocked on the wall between our bedrooms and I knocked back, I love you. It used to stop her having nightmares.

And I lay there congratulating the two of us, thinking how we'd done it, how a fat little shy girl from south London had won the lottery. I wish she'd let me show him the photos of when she was a little girl, but she wouldn't let me. I was so proud of her but she said he wouldn't understand, she said he would think that was the real her, a fat kid in shitty home-made clothes. That hurt.

I think she made a lot of stuff up, stupid things like pretending to have a different middle name. I called her Sally Karen, but she preferred Sally Anne. She never told him she

17

used a sunbed or that her dad had walked out before he got knocked down, daft little things really.

The car was coming to take her to the church at eleven. She didn't want any breakfast but I made her have a slice of toast in her dressing gown while the hairdresser rollered up her hair. She was going for an up-do, with a little diamanté tiara across the crown. Another girl did her face; she looked like something out of a magazine crossed with a cake. Skin so smooth it could have been caramel icing.

I zipped her up, admiring my overlocking as the satin closed snugly against her golden back, every seam sat just so. Ivory duchesse satin, there was just enough room to breathe. I'd measured her to the last millimetre.

The telephone rang at ten forty-five. Landline; we both jumped. It was Nick's father, he said there was a slight alteration to the plans and the car wouldn't be coming. Nick had changed his mind. He apologised as if he were calling off a lunch date and put the phone down.

I didn't have to tell her, she just said, 'I knew it. As soon as he found out about my middle name, he stopped believing in me,' and then she went into the kitchen, reached for the frying pan and fried herself bacon and eggs. She stirred up a tin of beans, put four pieces of toast under the grill and ate in her wedding dress. She ate like an animal, until the wedding dress was covered in greasy stains and bits of egg and bean and ketchup, and then she told me it was my fault.

There, that's that done. I've gone round the moon and taken two inches off the hem. She will be here in the next ten minutes, little miss perfect with her Bond Street breeding and no doubt suitable middle name, and I'm sure she and Nick will be very happy. After all, it's been three years since he jilted my daughter. I'm sure it's time we all moved on, only Sally can't seem to. She sits and eats and takes up space on my sofa and I know she's not well so I can't kick her out, but she never knocks on the wall any more, and I look at this dress and it's such a symbol of celebration I can't bear it. I can't stand how happy other people can be, and I think about her and Nick together, him holding bright, funny, uncomplicated little Imogen in his arms, and I think about my own daughter and how damaged she is and how I dread seeing her all spoilt now under rolls of blubbery unhappiness. And suddenly I am so angry I start to pull at the seams of the dress, and the tearing noise is satisfying so I pull at the sweetheart neckline until that rips too, and suddenly I'm in a frenzy of ripping and I reach for my scissors and I gash the skirt. I slice and chop it until I am exhausted and I look at my watch. She should be here by now. I told her I finish at seven. I stride over to the door, lock it and turn the sign to closed, and then I put what remains of the dress on a dummy in the middle of the shop floor, switch off the lights and hide in the corridor behind the shop. At five past seven she rings the bell, shakes the door handle and bangs on the glass, and then I hear her shout through the letter box, 'Maureen, it's me, it's Imogen,' and then I push the door to the shop a bit wider open and the light from the corridor floods the dummy and that's when I hear the crying. She howls and she wails and she screams 'Why?' and I hear her sobbing and it's like the dress is ripping all over again. With every wail my heart feels calmer. She cries and she cries until I am bored of her sobs and I creep out the back way and I go home via the Chinese takeaway to my fat unhappy daughter, and just maybe tonight I won't hear her sobbing through the wall.

3

Fantastic News

It's never easy, the first day, is it? First day anywhere really, school, new job, holiday?

John and I arrived last night, and it's a very nice gîte, in a very nice part of France, I think. To be honest, I'm not sure exactly where we are. We seemed to be driving down a narrow dirt track forever.

I knew we'd get lost because we didn't have a satnav in the hire car. Mind you, it wasn't automatic either, which is what John booked, an automatic with satnav.

John showed the man the paperwork at the airport but he just did that thing with his shoulders the way French people do.

They're good with their shoulders, aren't they?

I actually saw a French woman in the car hire place

balancing her jacket on her shoulders like you see in magazines. Now that sort of thing doesn't come naturally to us English women: if I tried balancing my jacket on my shoulders I'd lose it, or trip over it.

Anyway, it was a very fraught journey and John and I did a lot of swearing at each other. I may have called him an 'imbecilic shit', but then he might have called me a 'fat hysterical cow', so I think we're even.

To be honest, I feel a bit mean not going with him to the supermarket, which is either two roundabouts back and a left or three roundabouts back and a right.

We stopped off there on our way here last night, bought the usual basics: bread, wine, pâté, cheese – when in France and all that. John put a tin of frogs' legs in the basket for a laugh, but I took them out at the checkout. I'm not wasting good euros on scraggy old frogs' legs.

Let's just say that yesterday was a long day and normally we'd spend today relaxing and normally I'd have plenty of battery left in my phone because I don't make phone calls when I'm abroad, it's expensive. But I must have used all the juice up finding this place on Google Maps, which wasn't easy because I can't really see the screen with my glasses on and I can't really see it with my glasses off, so we were quite worn out by the time we got here, what with the flight being delayed by two and a half hours and the car hire business and the irritating woman with her jacket just so, and I bet she got the car we were meant to get – really, I could have given her a smack – so we just had some teeth-staining red wine and some cheese and bread and went straight to bed.

Not that I slept. Menopausal women in their fifties don't, we just lie there in a permanent state of semi-consciousness, like a shark. Or a bull frog, because they don't sleep either, they spend their entire lives wide awake and burping, which reminds me: I should have bought some Pepto-Bismol. Anxiety goes straight to my stomach.

I always keep my phone within reach when I go to bed because that's what you do when you're a mother. You're programmed to deal with any emergency that might arise in the middle of the night: 'Mum, I've lost my keys', 'Mum I'm at the police station', 'Mum, Martha's been sick and the cab driver won't bring us home unless you pay the soilage fee'.

Of course they're older now and neither of them lives at home. Scott is twenty-three and he's doing a BA, and Tamsin is twenty-nine, although you wouldn't think it because she's still painting her face with blue glitter and doing the festivals. Sometimes she does catering, a falafel stall, I believe, but really she's a poet, only they don't call it poetry any more, its 'spoken word', though hers is more shouted than spoken. Terribly sweary and very anti-establishment, which has caused a few problems, what with her father voting Brexit.

When Tamsin found out she said she'd never speak to him again, until John reminded her that he still pays her phone bill, so if she wasn't going to talk to him she wasn't going to talk to anyone – but apart from that, things have been quite calm recently, which is why I got very excited when I saw the text.

It woke me up, the tell-tale double beep, and instinctively I knew it was from my daughter. 'FANTASTIC NEWS,' she'd

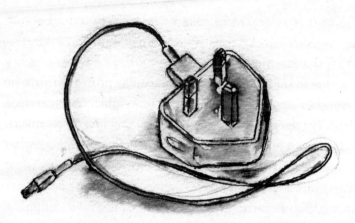

written, 'guess who just got engaged?' Then she'd added lots of exclamation marks and trumpet emojis and red hearts and a unicorn, but that's Tamsin, she loves a unicorn. In fact, she's probably got a unicorn dressing-up outfit.

She's the kind of girl who like a novelty hat: squirrels, rabbits, anything with ears really. I think it's time she was growing out of that sort of thing, but Tamsin believes in something called the power of play, which is a shame because she's a bright girl with a 2.1 in media studies from Sussex University. I hoped she might get a nice job at the local radio station as a reporter; she's got bags of personality. John always imagined her reading the weather on the six o'clock news, he's very interested in precipitation, is John, and he's right, she's got a lovely clear speaking voice and very elegant arms, just right for pointing at maps.

Anyway, as John says, the power of play is all very well, but it's probably why she's still living in a house-share in Forest

Hill with far too many bicycles in the hallway and green hair dye on every bath towel.

Then Tom came along.

I like Tom. I see Tom as a modern-day prince: I think he could save Tamsin from sleeping in tents and forever carrying a stinking sleeping bag around and getting lifts off strangers.

Tom has a job, a proper one – I can't remember quite what he does, I think its technical support for a big company, IT or something, or maybe it's HR. Anyway, he wears a suit and not a nasty, pop-it-in-the-washing-machine synthetic number, a proper suit, and from what I can gather he has a collection of ties and he's got a degree from a proper university – Warwick, where he did PPE.

And I know I'm rushing ahead of myself and John thinks I should calm down, but he didn't say no when I sent him off to the supermarket to get an adapter. Because after receiving that one little text, my phone died. One second there was a red line in the battery bar, the next, the whole thing just went blank.

'Just give it a charge,' says John, not that he'd bothered to charge his. Oh no, his was as dead as a doornail in the inside pocket of his second-best linen jacket.

So I fetched the charger from my tote bag but I couldn't find an adapter. I said to John, 'Where's the adapter?' He said, 'You usually bring the adapter,' and I do usually bring the adapter, but I got a new toilet bag for my birthday and I left the adapter in the old one.

So John has gone to the *supermarché* to find an adapter, and I told him if there's not one there he'll have to go all the way back to the airport to get one. I can't be in limbo like this; I need to know if Tom has popped the question. I know they've not known each other long, but six months is long enough when you're twenty-nine, because by the time you're twenty-nine there are a lot of short cuts you can take when it comes to relationships. You've had enough experience to know what you can and can't put up with. For example, Tamsin will never go out with another Virgo, but she doesn't mind vegans, not that Tom is a vegan. He's been round for dinner, I made my lamb – Greek-style, with the watermelon and feta salad; he was very complimentary. Apparently he's a foodie; Tamsin says he's a whiz in the kitchen – makes his own bread, not that she eats bread. She's gluten-free, but maybe Tom will bake her special loaves because that's what love is all about, isn't it? Doing nice things for each other, caring, and I hope John picks up some other provisions while he's at that supermarket, because if he comes home with just the adapter after going all that way I might have to kill him.

As we all know, the trouble with French bread is it goes stale. We need fresh bread and eggs, and I should have written him a list. That's the trouble with men of John's generation, they need to be told. John is very specific: if I say tomatoes, he says, 'What kind of tomatoes, big ones or those small ones?' I say, 'It doesn't matter, John, as long as they're nice. Just get me some nice tomatoes.'

That's all you want at the end of the day, nice, and *nice* may not be exciting and *nice* might not change the world, but I think Tom is a nice man, a good solid tomato of a man, adaptable but reliable.

He might encourage her to do that teacher-training course I've been banging on about. Tamsin would make a jolly good primary school teacher. All that enthusiasm needs harnessing to something practical; it would be such a relief if I could stop having to explain what she does in more than one sentence. If I could just say, 'Oh yes, Tamsin, she's getting married and training to be a teacher,' instead of endlessly having to make sense of why your daughter is almost thirty and had nothing to wear at her grandfather's funeral, not a decent pair of black shoes or a smart coat. I mean, leopard skin as an accessory is perfectly acceptable, but leopard skin when it's a great big matted floor-length nylon thing is not.

Still, she wrote a lovely poem, although I think we could have done without the words 'bastard cancer'. But fortunately a lot of the congregation were very hard of hearing and it's a shame my father didn't live to see his granddaughter walk down the aisle, but John and I will be there and we've got a bit of cash put by as long as she doesn't want anything out-landish – in fact, John might be able to get a discount at the golf club, they sometimes hire that out for receptions.

I can't wait to take her shopping for a dress. She's tall, so I think she needs something structured. I'm thinking a bit Kate Middleton, and no more than three bridesmaids. There's her cousin, of course, who can be maid of honour because she's already married. In fact, after I've spoken to Tamsin the next person I'm going to call is my sister, because – I don't want to be mean, but she was very smug about Jessica getting married at just twenty-four and all that guff about being sorry that Tamsin couldn't be a bridesmaid because she refused to take out her nose ring, and anyway all the other bridesmaids were under five foot five and Jessica wanted a uniform grouping. Tamsin said, 'Uniform grouping? Are they all going to be in matching tabards or something?' Which was a bit below the belt because, while Jessica does work for a well-known supermarket chain, she's in middle management with a company car and not sitting behind a till. Let's face it, you don't earn thirty grand a year and holiday in Mauritius if you're sitting behind a till. Last year Tamsin didn't earn enough to pay tax.

I just hope she doesn't want to do something silly like have an underwater theme. She's got a thing about mermaids, has Tamsin. I just want it nice, I just want it ordinary, I want a proper church organ and top hats and buttonholes. I don't want bits of seaweed draped everywhere and the theme tune to *Finding Nemo*.

I want a proper buffet with a selection of cold meats and fish, and some hummus for the vegetarians or cheese, and a marquee and a bit of a disco after. I want tears of happiness and a fancy three-tiered wedding cake that can double up as a christening cake, because they need to get their skates on with babies too. I don't want to be the oldest nana on the block, I want grandchildren while I've still got both hips and all my own knees. Ideally I'd like her to have two, because if anything happens to one of them she'd still have the other one to live for.

This is what it's like to be a mother. I want my daughter to share in the greatest gift that God and your ovaries can give you.

Because children are a gift, even if every sinew of your heart is worried sick every minute of every day, even though there's a lot of upset and expense and disappointment. Yes, disappointment like when she failed her grade three piano, when I was convinced she was good enough to play professionally. Nothing beats a mother's love, it is unconditional; a mother's love transcends everything, even the fact her nose has always been a bit pig-like and the ring only makes it worse.

For heaven's sake, where is that bloody useless man? Dear God, I tell you if he's forgotten which side of the road he's supposed to be driving on and got himself killed, I will never forgive him, because I want my daughter's wedding day to be the happiest day of her life, not a big tear-stained damp patch of a day because her father's dead. Honestly, John, and then I hear the car.

I only had to charge the phone for ten minutes before I got another text – it was from Tamsin. Jack and Milo, isn't that fantastic? I don't know who Jack and Milo are. I don't care about Jack and Milo, I care about my about-to-turn-thirty daughter, and suddenly it dawns on me that it may never happen: I may never see my daughter walk down the aisle on her father's arm and she might end up living in rented accommodation for the rest of her life and I may end up grandchildless, which is ridiculous considering I have all the skills, like knitting and bun-making, and then I smell something and I find John in the kitchen and he is slicing up tomatoes. Nice tomatoes, still a bit green around the edges, and he is frying them for breakfast and he has bought French bread and proper coffee and apple juice because orange juice gives me wind, and I realise that I am a very lucky woman and this realisation makes me cry and cry and cry, and John says, 'Did you remember your HRT, love?'

4

Beverley in Shoes

Trick is not to look at the clock. I've got a tea break in fifteen minutes, nice, take the weight off the old plates. Been slow this morning: a four-year-old by the name of Joe, last few scabs of chicken pox crusting over on his face, needing a new lace-up, very narrow fitting; three-year-old girl, tiny bit of a madam, knew exactly what she wanted, a pair of red leather Mary Janes; and a mum buying replacement gym pumps, second time this term, kids have no idea about the cost of anything, have they? And it's always us mums picking up the pieces, trying to make it better.

I've cross-checked some deliveries, read my horoscope, tidied the stock room, made some orders. I like working in a department store, it suits me.

I used to work on the cruise ships – dancer, it's not that

different. Soon as you're on the floor and the doors are open it's show time, you're what I call 'on'. I mean, no one expects me to do a cha-cha-cha through blinds and curtains with a pineapple on my head, but I could. I still wear a small heel – I can't do flat. Some of the women that work here are very puffy around the ankle, fallen arches, blue veins like motorways running up the backs of their legs. I might have put on some timber over the years but I think you can forgive a big bottom for a trim ankle. I've always had nice legs and a high kick. As my grandma would say, 'If you can kick a copper's hat off then there'll always be a place for you in the chorus.' I used to do a lot of ballroom, Latin, course it's very popular these days, what with *Strictly*. I wish I'd looked after my costumes better but I left them up in the loft, all mouldy and eaten by mice, all that tulle and a million sequins. I'm surprised there wasn't glitter in the droppings. Should have spotted it, but you get distracted, don't you? Life, eh? The second you look the other way it's *bam*.

Funny really, I spent years fearing the worst, but then when it happened it was still a shock, sheer blind panic. I knew as soon as I heard the phone.

Maybe that's why I need all this order. Helps you breathe easier when you know everything's organised. There's not a speck of dust on these shelves, they're clean, proper clean, right to the back and round the corners, be nice to live here. Sometimes, when I can't face the idea of that stinking bus journey home, I think about hiding in the ladies' toilets and having the place to myself of a night time. Imagine, all the time in the world to try on hats and browse the lingerie. I got myself measured here, fourth floor – you want Lorraine, she's an expert. Turns out I'd been wearing a 36C when all these years I've been a 34D. That's why I couldn't be a proper dancer, ballet, I mean. By the time I was fourteen my dance teacher said to my mum, 'Your Beverley's going to have a bosom on her and there's not a minimiser in the world that's going to make a jot of difference.' So we swapped to ballroom. I've won silver cups big enough to bathe a Labrador in, more rosettes than Shergar.

Imagine it, all night. I'd help myself to posh chocolates, light a scented candle and curl up in one of the display beds. New sheets – nothing like them. I mean, I wash mine every other Thursday, but I can never get them looking like new. I like the bedding department, I like all the fancy throws and cushions. I'm cushion mad me, good job I get a discount. They're a very good company to work for, and I can always nip over to ladies' perfumes for a squirt of something posh behind my ears if I'm going somewhere nice after work. Not that I go out much any more. Funny, isn't it, you spend half your life sailing round the world and the other half sat in front of the telly with a lap-safe tray watching repeats of *Doc Martin*. I can't watch anything violent any more. I don't want blood and explosions, I don't want bodies and people hurt. I like *Call the Midwife* and watching people make chutney.

Lots of perks to this job. I'm a fiend for a tester, I've tried every kind of collagen cream for the neck and décolleté. That's the trouble with being an ex-sunbather: 'fine lines and wrinkles', it says on the packaging – what about great big creases? Honestly, I'm like something out of World of Leather.

I've always liked shopping. Whenever the ship docked, me and some of the other girls would be first off, visiting the markets. Tunisia and Morocco, all embroidered slippers, hookah pipes and leather bags that smelt of cow dung – first floor for handbags and belts here, women's accessories, sunglasses. I spend some of my breaks with Gail and Anissa – Greek girl, dab hand with a silk square. People think accessories is a breeze but there's a lot of time-wasters and people just passing through on the way to use the conveniences. Don't get me wrong, I'd rather work in accessories than down in kitchenware, but I think I could get quite snappy.

Anissa says there's a lot of dithering and women saying 'I'll come back later' then disappearing off the face of the earth, and you've got to watch out for the tea leaves. Some folk are like magpies: if it's small and sparkly, they just can't help themselves. Anissa told me she once turned a blind eye: fifteen-year-old girl wanted something for her mum, couldn't afford anything Anissa showed her, nicked a bracelet. Gail said, 'I'd have cut her hands off,' which is a bit over the top, but then Gail's no-nonsense. That's why she's down in the basement, electrical appliances, there's nothing she doesn't know about a steam iron. Have you seen them these days? They look like speedboats, they come with their own launch pads. Takes me back, Sardinia, the French Riviera.

Gail plays netball, experiments with gluten-free cakes on her day off. I'm afraid she's yet to persuade me of the culinary merits of polenta, and anyway, I like to watch my figure.

There's a dress code in store, but it's not that strict. I keep it simple, black mostly, and I need to be able to bend down

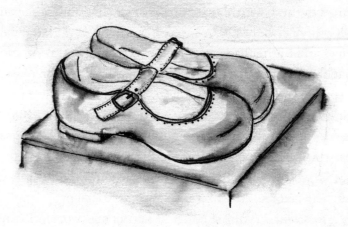

without showing the tops of my tights. I've got a couple of calf-length swirly jersey skirts – I'm not big on trousers, but when you've to do a lot of kneeling and crouching you've got to be practical.

Children's shoes, that's me, third floor. Prams, nursery furniture, haberdashery, children's wear and toys. The dancing helps; I think it's more appropriate to be able to get up and down without your knees clicking or too much grunting. I'm not saying there's a test, but if there *was* a physical some of our shop-floor ladies wouldn't pass. There are some quite big girls – not mentioning any names (Connie in stationery). We have a 'fun with flexibility' class before work on a Wednesday morning, and well . . . some of them are as flexible as a frozen leg of lamb. There's a lot of laughing, a lot of mucking about and I'm grateful for it, what's that word – camaraderie.

Obviously we have our very busy periods – just before a new term, Christmas – but between times we tick over. It's one of the things in life you can rely on: kiddies' feet grow. Shame really, not many grown-ups have nice feet. Mine are knackered, ruddy great bunions, and for years I pretended to be a six when I was a seven. Never went out without a padded plaster in my handbag. But a child's foot, there's nothing so perfect. I like the little ones, come in for their first proper shoes, the toddlers all dribbly and proud of themselves like no one's ever thought of standing up and walking before.

It's a science, fitting shoes. It's all about the bones. A baby's born with twenty-two bones in each foot, and by the time they start school it's gone up to forty-five. Forty-five tiny soft bones, like a sardine! Course, over the years these bones start to strengthen and fuse until you're about eighteen, at which point the fully mature adult foot has twenty-six bones. That's why you've not got to squash them: a child's shoe has to be soft but supportive.

And some people just don't get it. Ooh and it makes me mad. I blame the internet, apparently there's a measuring app you can download onto your iPad. Imagine. You get the kid to stand on the iPad and, presuming it doesn't break, this app will measure the length and width and then, hey presto, you've got your shoe size! Now don't get me wrong, I know more than most what a brilliant thing technology is and I thank the boffins and the brainboxes every day of my life, but if there's one thing that's best left to a middle-aged woman on her knees in a department store, that's fitting a kiddie's shoe, and to be honest it's about the only thing I am prepared to get on my knees for. It's not that I don't want to meet someone, but I just haven't the energy. Love is so tiring, isn't it? The worry of it.

Five minutes to break time. Sandy will cover for me. Sometimes I get a girl come in with a promising ballet foot – nice high arch, good turn-out, automatic point, slightly muscly calf – and I remember all my old ballet shoes. The pink satin, stitching on the ribbons, I was on pointe for a bit. Course you get some right trotters and all. Kids with feet like Monster Munch, stinking of cheesy Wotsits, verrucas and hammer toes. Seen a kiddie with webbed feet once, told his mum it was lucky – well, you never know. 'He'll never drown,' I told her, and I hope that's true, cos you can't always be there to save them. Soon as they get their first pair of shoes they're off.

I shouldn't have been surprised when Neil joined the army – he was a sucker for the advertising. 'I want to see the world, Mum.' I said, 'Join the cruise ships, be an entertainer.'

You don't need to join the army to see the world. You never go anywhere nice: Camp Bastion, wind and sand. Big army boots, ugly, never got used to seeing them, horrible things, bone-crushing. Eighteen when he signed up, feet only just fully formed, never had a dad to stop him. I did a daft thing on a stopover in Kefalonia, by the time we got back to Portsmouth I was puking up every morning. Thought it was seasickness, nine months later it turned out to be a ten-pound baby. Black curly hair, just like his dad's . . . I think. I've been in retail ever since.

Long feet, my lad, size eleven. Clumsy and all, always tripping up. If anyone was going to step on a landmine it was Neil. They're not even there any more, the British army, just a few of them left training the Afghan military. Camp's all bulldozed, what a waste. He thought he could still feel it, that's what he told me, said he couldn't believe he'd lost it when he could still wiggle his toes.

Right, break time. I can smell Sandy before I can see him, terrible BO. Nice lad, mind, lives with his mum. He's never going to get his leg blown off.

Left leg below the knee, his mates carried him back to camp. Could have been worse, but for a while it was touch and go. That's why I like coming here, I feel safe. The rest of the world can be going bonkers but not in here, no blood and sand, we don't even have music in the lifts. It's calm here, peaceful, and you can get a lovely cappuccino in the espresso bar on the sixth floor.

I should really take the stairs but I'm meeting Naomi, Neil's fiancée. She's coming up from Stanmore to meet a girlfriend for lunch, says she'll stop by and have a coffee with me first. I've a lot to be grateful to Naomi for, she's stuck by him, all those months of depression, physio. I used to think he could do better but I was wrong, he's lucky. She's got shocking feet, mind. Very broad, Naomi's feet, solid and waxy. She likes a Birkenstock in summer, big yellow toes, nails like rhino horn, chipped nail varnish. Capable girl, mind.

The café's behind stationery. I give Connie a wave, but I'm not stopping. I don't want to keep Naomi waiting.

It's a terrible thing when your child doesn't want to live,

when all they want to do is curl up in a hole and disappear. She's been like superglue, has Naomi – though she could do with wearing a bit more make-up. I've offered her a makeover for her birthday, there's a woman called Tina on the Clarins counter downstairs can do miracles, but she wanted a soup-maker. Funny girl.

There she is, tucked away by the window. Honestly, what is she wearing? Looks like she skied here. That's one terrible anorak, but I'm not going to say anything. She motions for me to sit while she gets me a coffee; I mouth 'Cappuccino, no sugar,' and I sit down at the little table she's chosen in the corner and there's an envelope with my name on it so I open it up and for a second I'm not sure what it is, a black-and-white photograph with all fuzzy bits. Maybe it's upside down. And then it hits me, it's a baby, a scan of a baby, and on the back it says 'Thought you'd like to know'. Neil's handwriting, letters all wonky, and I turn the picture over and I drink it all in, the big round tummy and the massive head, the curled fists and tiny wishbone legs and the paddling feet. My grandchild is swimming before it's even born and the pride and the hope that spring up in me, I don't know whether to laugh or cry, so I do a bit of both and I'm going straight to haberdashery at lunchtime and I'm going to get me some wool, and I might never have knitted in my life before but it's time I learnt because I'm having a grandchild and the first thing that baby's going to need is a pair of booties.

5

Christine Paints

It was Tony's idea to move to the country and I do love it, though the commute is a bore. But, as Tony says, 'You only do four days a week now, Christine, and Oxford's not a million miles from London.' In any case, he promised to give me a lift to the station every morning and he did until he lost his license, and now it's all a bit complicated, but I manage it. He was so mortified, but as he said, it's not easy, just nipping out for a pint when you're in the middle of nowhere. Luckily he only got a six-month ban. So really, it's not such a big deal.

Tillingholme might not be the centre of the universe, but we wanted a bit of peace and quiet so that Tony could write and finally, after two years, he thinks he might have something, only he's not sure if it's a novel or a play and he won't show me in case I jinx it.

Tony was an actor when we first met, but he never got the big break, which has been hard, especially when some of the people he was at drama school with have done quite well. We turn the telly off if one of the *lucky ones* turns up.

I work in HR for a large charitable organisation, but really it's very boring, so I'm glad we've downsized and I've cut my hours. It's not like we have to worry about children. Thank goodness for small mercies, that's what I say.

Tony sometimes gets a bit claustrophobic in the cottage. He finds the ceilings very low, but that's a seventeenth-century thatch for you. It's actually very pretty, in a chocolate-box kind of way. Tony wants a studio built in the garden, quite a few people round here have that sort of thing. There's money in the area, lots of converted barns and glass extensions. I've said maybe next year. Because let's face it, I've already had the expense of a new car this year, after Tony put ours in a ditch.

I thought we could just make do with a cheap little run-about but we got a bit carried away in the car dealership and I've ended up with a convertible – which is actually rather fun. You only live once and all that.

I have to say, there are lots of perks to working part time and living in the country, apart from having to buy all our weekly food from the train station, because as Tony says, he can't write a novel and/or a play if he's going to spend half his life waiting for a village bus to take him to the nearest butcher's.

Fortunately there is a Marks at Paddington, though Tony keeps talking about growing our own veg. You get a lot of garden for your money here – ours is mostly covered in rotting apples at the moment, a great big maggoty carpet of them. I've made some chutney but it isn't very nice, and Tony's not eating puddings at the moment so that's a no to apple pie or crumble. It's just a shame to see them all full of wasps and caved in, it's such a waste. Tony was going to make cider, but he seems to have gone off the idea. He gets his wine delivered now. Well, it makes sense, there's not a late-night offy for miles. I don't miss Kentish Town, but I think Tony does. He says he misses the culture, the theatre and the galleries, but I think he misses being able to nip out at 2 a.m. to get some fags.

Anyway, I can't remember the last time we did anything cultural together. Besides, I'm still going to London, I go four times a week. He could always come into town with me but really there's no need, there's plenty of activities around here, you just have to get involved. I do a Friday-morning art class, beginners' watercolours. I thought it would be a nice thing to do together so we went into Oxford and I spent a fortune on paints and paper. Tony wanted to get an easel, but I thought we should wait and see if easels were provided and they are. We've got a two-hour slot in the church hall, after the over-sixties' Zumba. Tony says maybe I should give that a go too, but I'm not sixty and anyway, I'm not the one that's put on two and a half stone since we moved. That's why he's off the puddings: it's like someone blew him up with a bicycle pump. He says fresh air makes him fat.

He's been to the class a couple of times but he thinks it's all a bit slow. He got bored with the rules of perspective and finding your vanishing point; he said he didn't think Pollock or Warhol bothered with the rule of thirds or dynamic composition, they just threw paint around, and in any case, he felt watercolour was the wrong medium for him and he felt more drawn to oils. I think he might have used the word visceral.

Hugh is our teacher, very patient. We're a mixed ability group: there's a couple who've been coming for years, an old boy, retired, must be knocking on eighty, likes a seascape – we call him the Turner of Tillingholme – and his wife who does a lovely cloud formation. Skies can be very therapeutic. Hugh says, 'Don't be scared of the paper, it's only paper. Plenty of water, that's another trick, load your brush.' He wears a funny little denim hat, like Donovan used to. Tony says he's an idiot.

We have a charity exhibition every six months, for a local school, special needs kids, cheese and wine and a blues band.

I wish Tony was in the blues band, but he's not found it very easy to make friends. It's because he's that bit younger, a lot of people round here are retired and Tony's young for his age. He's fifty-four but he keeps quiet about it.

Most of us do two paintings for the exhibition. People are very generous – as I say, there's plenty of money round here. Tonight's sale is hosted by Bella Cheeseman, because we've had an asbestos disaster at the church hall and it's closed for the foreseeable. So Mrs Cheeseman that was – divorced, bit of a looker – has very kindly stepped in because she's got a long barn in the garden that used to be her ex-husband's recording studio, and now she uses it for pilates and, well, us. I think she's drawn the line at the over-sixties' Zumba and I don't know where the Brownies are doing their thing, but for the time being we have a new temporary home and the views are spectacular.

Bella has an extraordinary figure; she's sat for us a few times. I think she likes taking her clothes off, she's very casual about it. Well you would be, if you were size twelve with year-round tan lines. She's what I call very topiaried around a certain area.

I have to say, someone's done a very nice job on her barn conversion. It's very swish, guest accommodation at the far end, bedroom, kitchenette and en suite, which is useful because it means none of us have to tramp into the house to use her loo.

I think she's hoping the exhibition will mostly feature herself in the nuddy and all the male villagers will struggle to hide their priapic excitement.

She's two teenage sons, so you'd think she'd know better, but then maybe if I'd looked like that in my late forties I'd have wanted to flaunt it.

She's hired caterers. Normally we all just contribute something, sausage rolls and homemade curry puffs, but apparently she's doing sushi.

We get a bit giddy on exhibition night. Everyone makes a bit of an effort to dress up and no one knows who's chosen what to put up. All I know is mine will be hung last minute because it's a Thursday night and I'm coming straight from work. I went into the office semi-gladragged this morning and added a bit of sparkle in the ladies' loos before I left.

I've got my paintings in the back of the car. One's the sunset I've been working on for the past couple of weeks. It's from a photo, but Hugh doesn't mind that, he says, 'Whatever inspires you is fine.' The other one is very simple, pen and ink and a bit of wash. The only bit of colour in it is a scarf, a yellow paisley scarf.

I saw it on the bed in her guest room when I used the bathroom last week. It was on the floor by the side of the hastily made bed. I knew it was Tony's, I bought it for him. I picked it up and gave it a sniff, grapefruit body wash, Silk Cut and red wine, my husband's signature scent, and the relief was overwhelming.

Tony's helping to hang the paintings. 'Not mine,' I said, 'I'll be bringing mine from work. I'm taking them in to show the girls.' He sort of rolled his eyeballs at that; Tony doesn't really understand how it feels to be fond of work colleagues and how sometimes you want to say goodbye.

Because I'm not going back and I haven't even told him. He'll find out soon enough.

Last time we had a show I sold my *Oranges in the Moonlight* for a hundred and fifty pounds and my *River Walk* for seventy-five, which was a tad disappointing, though I have to admit, some of my ducks looked a bit mutant.

I always give my painting titles. I think 'untitled' is very lazy. As they say, every picture tells a story, and the least you can do is give the person looking at it a clue.

I've decided what I want to call my sunset, it's just the other one that's bothering me, but I'm sure I'll come up with something before we kick off, which is in about five minutes.

Bella's going to be giving a speech. I think it should be Hugh, after all it's his class, but as he says, 'If Bella hadn't given us a home, we wouldn't have a class.' He's very generous like that.

Judging by the number of cars parked up, it looks like a good turnout. I'm not sure how Tony will have got here. Maybe he's been here all day, helping.

Right, let's get these paintings indoors. I made sure I wrapped them up safely in a blanket, we don't need anything else to break, a marriage is enough. It's odd, I feel quite calm. Here we go, I can creep in through the back door.

Hugh has saved me some hanging space at the end of the far wall. I'm next to Lillian Gilmour's *Radishes* and *Gino Sleeping*, which is a portrait of her very old dog.

I spot Tony on other side of the room. He's looking very smart and Mrs Cheeseman seems to have roped him in as a wine waiter. Bella's gone full arty, ripped jeans, boho embroidered blouse, glimpse of a fuchsia-coloured bra.

I put my sunset up first, pleased with the way my colours bleed down from the sky into the sea and onto the sand. It's possibly one of the most abstract things I've ever attempted. Hugh was thrilled, apparently I'm 'letting go', and I am. I'm letting go of all the things I no longer want in my life, including the job that has bored me for the last thirty years, but which I had to do because my husband was *too creative* to work.

I stick my label with the title *Future* next to my sunset, and as Bella walks to the microphone I unwrap the second picture and hang it next to my sunset. As I straighten it up and step back, Bella is tapping on the microphone and everyone obediently stands still and hushes for the speech.

Apart from Tony, who begins to make his way towards me. His expression changes with every step. The closer he gets, the more he recognises himself.

I have drawn Tony naked. The flab of his belly and the fold of his double chin are in repose. He is sprawled on an unidentifiable bed and I may have been mean with the proportions of his manhood, but no doubt Bella knows the truth. He is unshaven and unsightly, bloated and washed up. The yellow scarf lies crumpled on the floor, next to an empty bottle of wine. It's the only bit of colour in the piece, I wanted it to stand out. I wanted them to know how I knew, the sheer carelessness of it. My husband wasted our marriage and now he is pushing his way towards me with a real sense of urgency, but his progress is hampered by the fact he still has a tray full of drinks in his hands and people are stopping him. After all, rumour has it Bella has provided a particularly nice Chablis, and before Bella starts speaking I seize my chance. It's seven o'clock and I slip out of the door leaving my husband reading the title to his portrait, a title which simply reads *Past*.

Outside, he is waiting by my car. We've had this planned for a while now. I am running away with Hugh, we are going to live in Tuscany, we are going to buy a villa and Hugh will teach art and I will . . . I will enjoy myself, and I wish I could say we were driving off into a beautiful sunset like the one I've just hung in the barn priced at one hundred and twenty-five pounds, but unfortunately its dark and a bit drizzly, but as I make my way over to a man in a funny denim hat I have never felt happier. Behind me, I hear a crash. It sounds like someone may have dropped a tray of drinks, but I could be imagining things.

6

A Trolley for a Change

I don't normally come here, I usually go to Morrisons or the Co-op, but there's more choice here and the quality's better. Pricey, mind, makes your eyes water, but you've got to push the boat out now and then. Thing is, it's making me confused, not knowing where anything is. I'm going round in circles and I forgot my list.

I had it all organised in my head: make a nice shepherd's pie, everyone likes shepherd's pie, you can't go wrong. I'm good with mince, years of practice. Thing is, I can't do much else. I watch these cookery programmes on the telly and it's like watching magicians. But then I thought, maybe a shepherd's pie is a bit boring for the kids, they probably get that sort of thing for school dinner, so I thought I could do a buffet. Nothing fancy, just some sandwiches and a few treats, maybe a quiche I could cut up. I wish I knew what they liked. That's why the buffet is a good idea, only I could have done with planning it out. Sandwiches are easy, egg mayonnaise and ham, and maybe something with cheese, cream cheese and cucumber. I can put little bowls of nibbles out, those posh crisps, olives.

I know Lauren likes olives. It's really very good of her to bring them round, but as she says she's got the car, and if traffic's on her side she reckons it's ninety minutes door to door from Southend.

Nice for the kids to grow up by the sea. Healthy, as long as they stay away from the arcades. I'm a sucker for a fruit machine, never know your luck. One-armed bandit – you're not kidding. I used take the train up and see them at their dad's place every other weekend, or at least once a month if he was busy, only Jason's been working up in Scotland for the past two years and, well, he couldn't take the children, so I've not seen as much of them.

I wish they'd stayed together, my son and his wife, not that I liked her. I thought she was hard, that Lauren, but she had to be. Jason was daft he chucked that marriage away, messing about. She wouldn't have it, and who can blame her?

Seven and nine now, the grandkids. Brown eyes from her side of the family. The photos in my purse are old and all tattered round the edges from getting them out. I've got more recent ones on my phone but it's not the same. I want proper photos.

Cocktail sausages, all kids like them, don't they? Ooh look, mini Scotch eggs. Two for one: that's more like it.

I've got a trolley for a change. I usually make do with a basket but I decided I'd do a big shop, get everything I need, and then I can pick up a cab from the rank outside and sod the expense.

My grandchildren are coming. Dairylea Triangles! Jason used to love them.

Busy here, Saturday morning. Lots of young families, dads too, babies in buggies. I like the little bald ones best, remind me of Jason when he was small. Mind you, he's not got much hair now. All the worry gives you a receding hairline.

'Excuse me . . . I said excuse me . . . ' Posh cow.

I tell you, the way some of the people in here just chuck things in their trolley. No checking the prices, great packets of smoked salmon, joints of gammon, anyone would think it was Christmas. It's not – but I won't see them at Christmas. Jason's going to be working – he's some kind of heating engineer in Glasgow – and Lauren and the kids will be spending the day with her parents in Billericay. They're nice enough, Mr and Mrs Mills. I met them at the wedding and at Barney's christening. I don't think they ever got round to having Ella done – who cares? Just more hat problems, christenings. To be honest, I don't bother God and God don't bother me. She was a big woman, Lauren's mum, that's what I remember. We had a long chat about the importance of a sturdy undergarment in the ladies' toilets; she said Debenhams did a very good range. He didn't say much, Frank – couldn't get a word in, mind, not with Heather rabbiting on. She sent me a letter after Lauren threw Jason out, said how sorry she was that Lauren and the children weren't going to enjoy the same kind of security that she and *her* children had enjoyed with *her* husband. Ooh you smug cow, I thought.

Mind you, no one can point any fingers at me: I'm a widow. It's no one's fault when someone dies. Fifteen years now, pneumonia, weak chest, rheumatic fever as a kiddie, no one's fault, just one of them things.

Barney was nine the other week. I sent him money and he phoned to say thank-you. I have to say, she's very good like that is Lauren – I could hear her prompting him, 'Say thank-you to Grandma.'

I heard him mutter 'What for?' 'The money,' she hissed, but it wasn't much and I don't think it was enough. They expect a lot these days and they can spot designer a mile off, sniff the difference between the knock-off market stuff and the real thing. Like these kids in here. You can tell the ones from the flats across the road, the kids whose mums have sent them out for burger buns and Frosties, little ones that can cross the road at five. Then you've got the posh kids, Mummy and Daddy's little darlings, all parcelled up in fancy coats, all the Oscars and Harrys, like little Tory ministers reaching for the boxes of cereal that costs four quid and don't even have a toy inside. What's all that about?

That's what I should do, I should get them a toy, a toy each. They've all sorts here, aisles of stuff, fancy stationery and lunch boxes, PlayStation thingies. Kids don't like money, they don't really know the value of it, but they like surprises, something to keep them amused.

It should be a bit like a birthday party this afternoon. We

don't need games, and I wouldn't know what they play these days. I used to try and do games at Jason's parties but all his mates liked playing was wrestling. There'd be me with my pass the parcel all wrapped up and ready to go, and they'd be running round screaming, trying to pull each other's heads off. To be honest, I really wanted a girl. He was hard work. E-numbers, food colourings and all that, that's what they used to blame it on. Now it's ADHD, attention-deficit disorder. Jason didn't pay attention to his wife, paid too much attention to some girl in a pub. Lauren finds out and boom, the whole thing goes up. What a waste.

Anyway, no good crying over spilt milk. That's another thing, what will they drink? I think Lauren might be too strict for Coke. I'll get some juice, not the juice drink stuff, the proper 100 per cent fruit stuff. Apple and orange, one of each and paper cups and straws. Jason would say 'Calm down Mum, you're going over the top,' but I don't get much chance to go mad. Ooh here we go, crisps – everyone loves crisps. I wish I knew which ones were their favourites. I used to like them Bovril ones.

I'm going to ask them loads of questions this afternoon and I'm going to write the answers down in a little notebook for future reference. Favourite flavour of crisps, best type of biscuit, what colour ice cream?

Which reminds me: freezer cabinets are at the far end and I mustn't forget bread. Be awful if, after all this, I forgot the basics.

At least parking at mine is easy on a Saturday. She won't need a resident's permit – good job, cos I've not got any – and the lift was working when I came down this morning. Still stinks of wee, mind.

They've not been to Grandma Pat's before. Eighth floor, if I was on the other side you could see Big Ben, but I'm round the other way, facing some more flats. I wish I had a park at the bottom with swings and slides, but I've not.

Anyway, she might not want me taking them out. She's only coming up because a mate of hers is in hospital. She's leaving the kids with me while she visits, then she'll be back to fetch them. To be honest, I wouldn't like to risk taking them out, I've not got the experience. I don't feel trained. I've got friends and they see their grandkids all the time. Unpaid childminder, my mate Wendy calls herself, but I've seen her with her mob and she can wipe a nose with one hand and stop a toddler from choking with the other, she's like a ninja nanny. But me, I've not got the confidence. Anyway, I think it's like gardening: some people have got green fingers, others are good with kids. I've not got either. I've a balcony full of dead busy Lizzies and I was a pushover with Jason – anything for a quiet life.

I don't know whether to do cake and biscuits, biscuits and pudding or pudding and biscuits. Jason liked Jammy Dodgers. I'll get a variety tin of biscuits, some mini rolls and a tub of ice cream, raspberry ripple.

Right, I've to get a wriggle on now. Cab home, quick tidy, open the windows – don't want Barney and Ellie to know Grannie Pat likes a fag now and again. Now and again my foot, I'm on fifteen a day and I'd have more if I could afford it, only I can't. I can't afford anything, so it's a good job I don't

56

see my grandkids too often. This recession has nearly done for me, four houses a week I used to clean and one of them was twice, so that was five shifts, two hundred quid cash in hand, can't argue with that. Only I'm down to two now; first thing to go when people are feeling the pinch, bit of help round the house.

Here we go, ice cream. I can't fit one of those big cheap tubs in my freezer, it's only a piddling thing. I'll have to get one of them smaller posh ones, never mind. I should have made a jelly, jelly's cheap, but I forgot to think. Oh come on, woman, get your skates on. Let's get out of here.

Pick the shortest queue with a cashier who looks like she knows what she's doing, not one of them gormless Saturdays lads, all dandruff and no idea. Here we go, this one, middle-aged, looks like she's looking forward to her lunch break. Bit younger than me, capable-looking, glasses and normal-sized nails. She might be a grandma too. It's like a club, only I feel like I haven't got full membership.

'Ooh, someone's having a party, anything special?' she says.

'Just the grandkids coming over.' I try and say it all casual, like it happens most weekends, even though there's a bit of me that feels like screaming, 'I don't know how to do this, I don't even know what to say to them, I don't know what class they're in or if they go to Brownies, I don't even know if they can swim.'

'Well, they're not going to go hungry.'

'They've got good appetites.' How do I know? I'm not sure they even eat butter. They could be allergic for all I know.

'I've got three, two girls and a boy. I'm babysitting tonight, as it goes.'

'We're just unpaid childminders.' See, she's not panicking, it's normal, looking after your own flesh and blood.

'Have you got a Nectar card?'

'No, no I haven't.' But I have got a bank card with about seventy quid left on my overdraft.

'Sixty-eight pounds fourteen pence, dear ... That your phone, love?'

'Oh yes, I can never find it in time.' That's cos no bugger ever rings it. I don't even recognise the tone. Stupid thing, all fiddly, I can't be doing with it. 'Here you go – my card.'

'Just pop it in the machine, love ... Ooh, there it goes again. Someone's just left you a message.'

'Nothing that can't wait, I'm sure.'

I hold my breath as I tap in my pin number – 1980, our Jason's date of birth – half waiting for the machine to spit it out, but it doesn't. I must have made it by a matter of pennies.

Luck is on my side and I heave all the bags into the trolley and in my head I'm whistling. It's going to be fine, the kids are going to be knocked out, they'll beg their mum to come and see me more often. Maybe next time they can stay the night. I push the trolley through Costa to the exit and out the automatic doors, and I'm looking for the taxi rank when this fella comes up, big bloke in a uniform, and he says, 'Excuse me, madam, would you mind coming back in the shop with me?'

I tell him I can't possibly, if it's all the same to him, because I'm in a bit of a rush today.

But he's got a hold of my trolley and he says, in a very calm voice, 'We just need to clear something up. It's just we have reason to believe you might have items about your person that haven't been paid for.'

I tell him I don't know what he's talking about and anyway, I can't stop, my grandchildren are coming, Barney and Ellie. I've got to get back to the flat, make it all nice.

But he's not going to let me go. He just shakes his head and he's not asking me now, he's telling me.

'I'm sorry, madam, but I'm going to have to insist.'

He got hold of my arm, he was very polite, tall, it was a bit like being escorted through an airport like a celebrity. Only then he takes me through the back, into the stock room, and I've to sit in this room and wait. There's a poster on the wall that says 'We always prosecute' and I feel sick. It was a DVD for the kids, *Despicable Me 2*, I thought it might take me over my limit.

He made me empty my handbag, old bits of tissue and a cough sweet stuck to the lining. My phone rolled out.

'Message received,' it said on the screen. When he went to fetch a pen I played the message back.

'Pat it's me, Lauren. Change of plan, I'm afraid. We're not going to make it this afternoon. My mate's being discharged today so there's no point. Sorry, Pat, another time – I'll give you a bell in the new year.'

And I sat there waiting for the police to turn up while that posh tub of ice cream turned to mush.

7

First Impressions

I met Belinda at the gym. I decided to treat myself to membership when Bellamy and Conran saw fit to terminate my employment. My mum said, 'What's wrong with the leisure centre?' But I know someone who went there and got athlete's foot on her *face* from using a filthy communal yoga mat.

Anyway, the way I see it, no one's going to take you seriously unless you take yourself seriously. Don't get me wrong, I've got a GSOH, but some things just aren't really laughing matters, like being over ten stone and needing your upper lip waxing.

See there's a lot of competition out there, hundreds of thousands of us, gone thirty-five, hovering under forty. My mate Pete says you can smell the desperation on women my age. Reckons it's even worse for gay men. Pete says, once you hit thirty-six you might as well be dead.

We have a laugh, me and Pete, but then he goes one Jägerbomb over and he's trying to get off with Uber drivers. Or anyone really, but mostly Uber drivers, because basically he wants someone to drive him home and then come indoors and keep him company.

We all get lonely.

Anyway, she's a very nice woman, is Belinda. I'm not going to start slagging her off now, just because tonight's turned out like . . . Well, not how I saw it in my head.

I'm a romantic, I like pictures of honeymoon beaches and sometimes when I can't get to sleep at night I design my wedding cake in my head. Last year it was all individual cupcakes, but I've gone off that.

Sometimes my mum says to me, 'By the time I was your age I was married with three kids.' And my dad says, 'Leave her alone, Sal, she's a career girl.'

Only I'm not, but even if I was I don't think it's fair. I don't think that just because you're a woman means you've got to go through life sacrificing one thing for another.

Though sometimes you do, obviously. Like if you want to stay a size twelve then you can't come indoors of a night time and eat a load of cheese, not unless you want to spend the next three days doing spin classes.

Belinda is in very good nick. Tonight she's wearing white trousers and a cropped top – that's a lot of sit-ups. She's got a personal trainer and she does group classes too; I just do some stuff in the gym that I've made up myself and group classes. I haven't got the cash for one on one.

Belinda has Stephano on Wednesdays. He's the best,

everyone says so – even me, though I've never actually had a session with him. It's just one of things that everyone knows.

I started bumping into her in the changing rooms, watched her getting changed. Not in a weird way, it's just some women, well, let's just say there are women that go to my gym, turn up in fancy cars and then you see them in the changing rooms and they're wearing bras that look like they found them on a night bus. All stray pubes, frayed knickers and yeti armpits.

I've always done matching. Well, it's all about presentation, isn't it?

I might not have the best boobs, and I know for a fact that my legs aren't all that cos I once went out with a bloke who gave them a four out of ten, but I make sure I keep my tan all year round, gels on my toenails, and I've had my bikini line permanently lasered. Makes sense, no regrowth or embarrassing ingrowing hairs. I'm not saying I used to get boils around my hairline, but I did and that's never going to work, is it?

The thing is, you've got to be ready, like an athlete, because you never know when it's going to happen. That's why I don't mind spending a hundred quid on a bra, because one day it's going to pay off.

I've got friends who are married and they've stopped bothering. Well, that's fine, they're married, they can spend the rest of their lives on the sofa in elasticated jogging bottoms, but the fact is you don't start from there, you start with a toned tummy and professionally blow-dried hair. You begin with expertly plucked eyebrows and a face that you have looked at a million times in a massive pore-magnifying mirror so that you know how best to disguise it.

You learn how to apply your make-up to accentuate your eyes and draw attention away from your nose, which is too long and too fat, and you know exactly which shade and make of lipgloss will make your lips look enticing but not like they're going to make a big sticky mess all over his face. Mine's Long Last Glosswear in Tenderheart by Clinique; it costs £16.50.

It is expensive being single. About five years ago I went to eleven weddings in twelve months. They've calmed down now, everyone's done it – some of them have been there, done that and are getting divorced. I don't buy wedding presents any more, I just email the happy couple and tell them I'm donating an unspecified sum to a charity on their behalf. You never get an email back saying, 'You lying cow, I bet you're spending the money on yourself.'

Of course I am, it's payback time. Muggins here is the one that ends up paying the single-room supplement every time I have to stay in a hotel.

And no, I'm not going to bunk up with a mate, I'm not fourteen, and anyway, the only time I did that the girl in question, woman rather, tried it on with me in the middle of the night and I had to threaten her with my hair straighteners.

Anyway, Belinda's married – and, as far as I can see, quite happily – to Alex, who she sometimes refers to as 'sweetie'.

'Sweetie, JoJo hasn't got a drink,' says Belinda.

I'm JoJo, by the way. It makes me sound rather more fun than boring old plain Joanna. JoJo is the life and soul, especially when she's had a couple of Alex's margaritas.

'Just a kitchen supper,' she said, 'to christen the new kitchen.'

Yes, Belinda is the kind of woman who can ask sweetie for a new kitchen and she will get one, complete with acres of Italian marble and under-floor heating.

We became proper friends when I found her rings in the showers at the gym and made sure she got them back safely, a plain gold wedding band and a sapphire engagement ring.

I tried them on, but they were rather tight. In fact, I had a rather panicky five minutes with a lot of soap before I handed them in at reception. She tracked me down, wanted to thank me personally, bought me a smelly candle.

I now realise it's probably one she got from her cleaner for Christmas; she's strictly a Jo Malone Lime, Basil and Mandarin girl in the home. This was cheap, sweet and cloying; it smelt like burnt sherbet.

Anyway, we're really good mates, sort of. She feels safe, because girls like me with big noses don't impose any real threat and she likes the way I don't try to hide how jealous I am of what she's got. I tell her, 'You're a lucky cow, Belinda,' and she laughs because she knows she is, and because we are such close friends she shows me the little bruises on the insides of her thighs.

Belinda and Alex have a very vigorous sex life.

I make jokes about my best friend being my vibrator. Which isn't true: I haven't got a vibrator and my real best friend is actually called Laurel, but she went to live in Melbourne with an Australian bloke that we met at a house party in Beaconsfield.

Which isn't really fair, because I talked to him first, the Australian bloke, but I didn't really try very hard because I thought he was gay. Honestly, if I'd made more effort maybe I'd be eating grilled cuttlefish on St Kilda beach.

Not that I particularly fancy cuttlefish, but it crops up a lot on Laurel's Facebook. It's a craving – she's pregnant, of course. Her bump swells at the camera with increasing pride on a daily basis.

Belinda is always asking me about my love life. She's suggested all sorts: online dating, special introduction agencies, she even said I should pretend to drown in the pool when the quite nice-looking lifeguard is on duty.

But there's nothing sexy about pretending to drown, really, is there? It's all chlorine and snot, and anyway, if I do go swimming I usually wear a swimming cap because I've got difficult to manage hair and, well, it's not a good look.

She said, 'You're just going through a dry patch.' I said, 'Any drier and it'll form a scab and heal over.' Which I think was pushing it a bit far, because she just said, 'There's no need to be disgusting.'

I had to suck up to her for ages to get back in her good books, buying her chai soya lattes, making sure I always had a spare pound coin to lend her for the lockers, stroking her new Stella McCartney handbag as if it were a rare and precious animal. 'Hmmmm, how good this smells,' I said, and it does smell good. It smells of everything I want.

She eventually cracked when I told her about this new salon in town, where they've got a genius doing their threading.

I could tell she'd been, her eyebrows were immaculate and she's back on about this little dinner party. 'Friday,' she says, 'Max is going to stay at his grandma's.' I always forget she has a kiddie; there's not a stretch mark on her.

'Just a few close friends, neighbours mostly,' she says and then she plays her trump card. 'And Alex has invited Gavin.'

Gavin is a mate of Alex's. Anyway, he's single and he likes scuba diving and golf, and he works in hedge funds like Alex and they haven't seen him for a while, but now he's back on the scene, and if she had told me his surname I would have googled him right down to his DNA.

So I do the best with the information I've got. I read some stuff about scuba diving, like where the best places to go might be, and I look up PADI courses and things about coral reefs and giant squid. I want to make him feel comfortable.

I practise doing my hair in a way that takes at least a centimetre off my nose, only Belinda says 'What the hell have you done with your fringe? You look insane,' so I put it back the other way and come the big day I take care to eat sensibly, avoiding garlic and shellfish, just in case, and I start flossing my teeth around four, at one point I floss so hard my gums start bleeding and I have to be very careful not to have a panic attack. I bathe and shave and put on my hundred-pound bra – and matching knickers, natch – and the shoes that look like Louboutins even close up and a dove-grey wrap-around dress that only clings a bit and sometimes makes little crackling electrical noises, like fuses are going off all over my body, which I figure is the kind of thing some men like.

I have one small vodka at home to take the edge off, and wonder whether to hide the bottle in my bag, but the bag that goes with my outfit isn't big enough and I think about decanting some into a smaller bottle but then the cab comes and I just take one last big swig and I'm on my way.

In the cab I practise my silent breathing, because lately I've realised that sometimes I make a whistling sound out of my nose when I exhale, which is obviously a disgusting thing to do and what with him being a diver, Gavin will be a breathing connoisseur.

Belinda's house is in a gated community and is sort of old-fashioned but the brickwork is very clean and there's a proper gravel drive, which makes a noise like you're in a movie. I half-expected a maid to answer the door, only it's Belinda, all new caramel streaks and lots of silver bangles. She can't have cooked in those, I thought, all that clattering would drive you mad.

'Come through, come through,' she rattles and shrieks, and I realise she's nervous, as I would be if I ever owned that much cream carpet, what with the possibility of dog shit coming in on someone's shoe or red wine spillage.

She shows me through to a room overlooking a large garden: taupe walls; an abstract painting that might be Venice but could be a cross-section of the lower intestine; black leather sofas, the kind you have to be careful not to make fart noises on.

Two other couples are already clinking ice cubes and talking about traffic. An indeterminate mix of fat, ginger, bald and tall, a blur of handshakes and names. Gavin isn't here.

Belinda hands round crostini. I think they're from Waitrose, a classic luxury nibble mix, but she's arranged them nicely on a large square white plate.

I feel a yawn building along my jawline. There is no point in me being here if Gavin isn't coming; I might as well be at home drinking Chardonnay in bed with a box set.

Apparently we're having duck. Such a dark, sinewy meat, duck, no wonder it's always hidden inside a pancake and covered in jam.

'On his way,' she mutters, nudging me in the ribcage with

the crostini. I grab one so as not to appear rude, and shovel what is essentially an awkwardly shaped piece of toast into my overstretched mouth, only to realise the bloody thing is loaded with garlic.

Before I can nip upstairs to the master bathroom, where I suspect there will be an assortment of mouthwashes, the doorbell rings and seconds later I hear Belinda screaming 'Gavin!' from the hallway.

First impressions are very important. I haven't got time for blokes not to fancy me, until they get to know me and realise what a nice person I am, because I'm not.

I swallow hard, breathe in and my crostini-crumbed bosom strains against the intricate lace of the hundred-pound bra, which instantly proves its worth by creating a whopper of a cleavage. I dip my head so he doesn't notice my nose straight away and I lift my eyes.

He's very nice-looking, shorter than I imagined and not in his swimming trunks. He has a very good head of hair, as my mother would say, expensive jeans, a chunky designer watch which I bet he can wear in the sea when he's diving, a crisp white shirt, suede loafers and is holding a woman's hand.

The hand belongs to a young blonde wearing a flimsy skirt that dances like an old man's eye around her thighs. She is twenty-five, possibly even younger. The bored yawn starts to creep back along my jaw and Belinda refuses to look at me.

After a brief flurry of more names, handshakes and air-kisses, we are ushered through into the brand-new kitchen extension, full of fat cream roses and candles glinting on every surface.

The smell is overpowering. I should stop drinking, but the sight of This-is-Abigail's tiny nose and perfect teeth makes me reach for a chilled bottle of Chablis.

'Alex will see to your drinks,' trills Belinda, but I ignore her and fill my glass to the brim. Slightly over the brim actually.

About thirty minutes later I have duck smeared around my plate and plum jam down my grey silk bosom. Gavin is being hilarious about deep-sea diving and Abigail is clutching her tiny throat and saying how she could 'never dive in a million years'. I notice she doesn't eat the duck or the pancake, or the shredded spring onion accompaniment; she drinks water with her wine, sip for sip, and she has obviously bought some magical extra-shine shampoo that actually works. In fact, I wonder if she is the model on the bottle.

The plum jam stain is bothering me. It looks like a stab wound in my chest. I excuse myself and totter to the downstairs cloakroom.

Darkness has fallen and as I sit micturating, a word that simply means urinating (a fact I learnt at a singles' pub quiz night), I realise I can no longer bear to be in this house with these people. Fortunately the solution to my problem is blindingly obvious: there is a sash window behind the lavatory and the key to the lock lies tucked within the deep pink heart of a conch shell artfully balanced on the sink unit. I shall simply climb out of the window and go home.

I don't even bother to wash my hands.

Thanks to my recent lack of gainful employment and subsequent use of the gym's off-peak facilities, I find it quite easy to hoik myself over the lavatory and onto the Mexican-tiled windowsill, but as I drop down onto the flower bed below I realise I should have removed my fake Louboutins. Sadly it's too late and I land badly.

My ankle puffs up immediately, like a fat Yorkshire pudding in a twenty-denier stocking, as I begin limping across the lawn.

The pain is excruciating and I suddenly remember that I've left my handbag under the dinner table, my phone set politely to silent.

Frustration rises suddenly, taking me by surprise. My eyelids prick with tears of upset and temper. Quite simply, I am furious and drunk and as angry as I have ever been.

I wanted to get off with Gavin tonight. I wanted to show off my bra and do all the sex tricks I've learnt from women's magazines. I wanted to wake up in the morning and eat hot croissants with my new lover. Instead, I am destined to piss off my peculiar spareroom.com flatmate because I haven't got my keys, or my purse or anything, and she will do that thing where she pretends to be more German than she actually is and I long to get rid of her, but I can't afford to live in my flat unless a stranger sleeps in my sitting room.

The prospect of the long walk home makes me feel weepy, but the only other option is to spend the night on the back lawn in a child's plastic playhouse, which becomes horribly likely when I realise that the only way to the front of the house involves walking along a narrow path alongside the kitchen extension. I can't trust them not to have a security light. What would I say? 'Oh hello, I'm sorry, I fell out of the toilet window like a spectacularly shit Alice. I think I might have broken my ankle, would you happen to have any arnica, or failing that some amaretto? Yes, a nice glass of amaretto and maybe a lie-down on the sofa.'

Bollocks.

I can't climb back through the toilet window either, because the sash window dropped shut behind me and I'm not prepared to break every false nail prising the bloody thing back up.

So I do the only thing I can do: I find an ornamental wheelbarrow and push it up against the back wall. Climbing into it, I find that if I jump as high as I can while grabbing a steadying handful of ivy, I can just about launch myself across the wall.

It takes me seven goes and I graze both knees quite badly during this operation, but eventually I am lying horizontally along the wall, looking down at a pavement which is a dizzying nine feet below. Any mistake and I could conceivably break every bone in my body, in which case the consequent crawl home will be arduous in the extreme and there is no real guarantee that bad-tempered Brunhilde or whatever she's called will actually be around to let me in anyway.

For a while I just lie there, weeping brine into concrete grouting, the sound of a siren wailing increasingly urgently into my ear, until it suddenly stops screaming and I realise a police car is pulling up almost directly beneath me.

Finally the penny drops. The siren was responding to a concerned neighbour. Someone must have seen me attempting to get over the wall and called the police. Fucking ridiculous, what sort of intruder wears a knock-off Reiss grey silk wrap-around dress and a pair of five-inch heels?

The people round here deserve a good smack if you ask me, but no one's asking me anything. Two coppers get out of the car and sort of approach me, like I could conceivably have rabies, and one of them is sort of blond and quite good-looking and he's taller than Gavin, and in that split-second, as I lie here on my wall, I think, Well, why not? People meet each other in all sort of circumstances and maybe this is fate, and yes, I am quite pissed, but it feels like a fairy tale. He holds out his arms and, as elegantly as I can, with my bleeding knees and my puffy ankle, I fall into them.

8

Bones

Lydia is the apple of my eye. Lyd-i-a – even her name thrills me, I like hearing the sound of it rolling off my tongue. Such a pretty name, for such a pretty girl.

We are very close. I'm not going to say we're more like sisters or best friends because that's not what I am, I'm her mum. She's got a best friend called Lottie Miggin. I know, sounds like she should be working in a Victorian pie shop, but she isn't, she's a nail technician in Hackney. Has to wear a mask because of the fumes, toxic apparently. Lydia says Lottie gets terrible headaches, says she's chomping paracetamol all day long. I tell her, you've got to watch your over-the-counter pain relief. Stick to the recommended dosage or you can risk permanent liver damage.

Lydia works in Zara, gets a discount. She's got two Ikea

wardrobes, one in her bedroom, one on the landing, but she hasn't got a sister, or a brother for that matter, or a dad really. Just me, me and Lydia.

I did childminding when she was little, seemed the obvious solution. Course, there was a lot of wear and tear on my sofas, crayon up my walls, soggy half-eaten biscuits squashed into the carpet. At one point I had three potties on the go, which cost me a fortune in air fresheners. But I think it was good for both of us. I got some money and Lydia learnt to share: me, the house, her things. When she got older she helped me with the little ones; she never took to the bum-wiping but she was good at stories and cuddling, and letting them play with her old teddies. She's soft like that, is Lydia, still loves a cuddly toy and God knows how many cats we'd have if she wasn't allergic. Always buys the *Big Issue* and there's a busker outside our train station, only sings the one song. 'Wonderwall' over and over again, murders the thing. Seriously, if I were Oasis I'd sue, but Lydia, she'll always chuck him a bit of loose change.

'Lydia is a kind girl with a sweet nature', and I'm not just saying that cos I'm her mum; a teacher once wrote it on her report at primary: 'a kind girl with a sweet nature but she must learn not to let others take advantage of her'. I thought, What a load of tosh, she's nine. Then I found out she was giving her packed-lunch sandwiches to a big boy in the top class. I made sure she had school dinners after that.

As soon as she went to secondary school I went back to college, trained to be a nurse. I'm in A&E, Lydia doesn't know how I can stand it, blood and bone. The things I see, I tell you. There's a reason why nurses don't cycle in London. I wouldn't let Lydia have a bike for all the tea in China.

I've tried not to mollycoddle, but it's hard. There's an accident round every corner, stuff jumps out at you, ladders fall, cars swerve, lorry drivers lose concentration. Everywhere people are falling, bleeding, breaking elbows, wrists and chins, blood flows and pools, sticks and scabs, and in the middle of it, we stitch and mop and send them back out again. It's a war zone out there, stabbings and shootings on top of the silly stuff, the allergies to hair dyes, the six-inch-stiletto twisted ankles, adverse reactions to recreational drugs, the falling off of lamp-posts pissed. Sometimes it's the smallest accidents that do the most damage. You've got to watch out for the hairline cracks, the tiny little swellings and any strange skin discoloration. You develop a sixth sense: sometimes you just know that there's something else the matter, something buried deeper. That's when you call for scans and X-rays and keep your fingers crossed. Not that it helps, not really. Sometimes luck just runs out.

That's why you've got to be careful ... Stand back from the edge, look left, look right, look left again. I always say to Lydia, don't walk into trouble with your eyes wide open.

Soon as I get indoors I'm out of my uniform as quick as I can, cos at the end of a shift it stinks. That's the trouble with A&E, you're always in the firing line for a bodily fluid. Blood, pus, piss, sick, shit, you name it, I've come home covered in it.

Lydia smells of Molecule. It's a perfume, you can get it online. She loves her smellies; seriously, I've never known anyone get so much pleasure out of running a bath.

Christian buys her all that sort of stuff now. Her boyfriend, he's quite old-fashioned like that. When they first started dating he was forever buying her big bunches of flowers, and he still picks her up in his car from work when he can. He doesn't really like her using public transport, doesn't like the idea of strange blokes chatting her up. Bit jealous like that, is Christian.

I think she's too young to be settling down, but she says Christian's everything she's ever wanted. She says he's like her knight in shining armour, and that she can't wait to get married.

I was like that once upon a time. I think I ran up the aisle on my wedding day. I thought I'd bagged my happy ever after, but Lydia's dad snuck out on us before Lydia was even crawling; couldn't take the responsibility. Lives in Canada, apparently.

I think he talks to Lydia on Facebook. She's been very forgiving, but then that's Lydia. When she was about eight she said she thought it might be her fault that her dad left home. I said, 'You were a baby, how could it have been your fault?' And she said, 'Because I couldn't talk. If I could have talked I could have asked him to stay.'

Women often blame themselves, even when it's not their fault. Happens at work all the time. A woman can be run over on a zebra crossing in broad daylight, she can be lying all smashed up on a stretcher, drifting in and out of consciousness, and she'll still be apologising: 'I'm sorry, I'm such a nuisance. I'm so sorry.'

What is it with women? It's like we're hardwired to think everything must be our fault. Like being single, which is silly, but it's true.

The fact is, I wish I wasn't meeting Christian's parents on my own tonight, and I know there are millions of women in the same boat as me, but I'm sick of being in my boat. I'm sick of paddling away in this wretched one-woman kayak that could tip over any second and leave me gasping for air in freezing-cold water. OK, so I'm being dramatic, possibly because I don't really like these trousers, but I got chicken tikka masala down my good ones.

But there are times, and I hate admitting this, that I miss having a partner, a mate, someone who would make an effort for me, back me up, be on my side. He needn't be George Clooney, just a nice agreeable chap, who would polish his shoes and put on a clean shirt because he'd know, without having to be told, that tonight is important – that it means a lot to me to make a decent impression, for Lydia's sake. Seriously, I could do with some help here, because the responsibility is wearing me out. I want someone to share all the pride and the worry, someone I could turn to last thing at night and whisper, 'Really? Is he really good enough? What do you think? Can he make her happy, can he keep her safe?'

And it's not like these men don't exist, because I have seen them. Balding middle-aged men, ashen with worry, flying into the hospital, the husbands of the knocked-down women.

'Where is she, my wife?' I've seen the hand-holding and the tears sliding down the cheeks of fat fifty-year-old baby men. There is still a lot of love going on – I just didn't pick the right one. I picked a useless lump of rubbish and I couldn't even keep him.

Christian's mother used to play in an orchestra but she had to retire, something about her hands going stiff. Arthritis probably, it's a terrible disease. Christian's father is a chartered accountant. I'm not sure if there's a difference between a chartered accountant and a normal one, but anyway, Christian is following in his father's footsteps, which is sort of reassuring, because as Lydia says, Christian is very good when it comes to money.

Since they got engaged he's created a spreadsheet on his computer, income and expenses, that sort of thing, because Christian says renting's a mug's game and they need to economise if they're ever going to buy their own house. He's told Lydia that maybe it's time to stop paying Lottie to transform her fingernails into ten tiny watermelons, which I think is a shame, and I seriously don't think his idea of taking a flask of coffee to work to save on caramel lattes with chocolate sprinkles is going to work either.

She says it'll be worth it in the end, but I saw her face drop when Christian bought her a tiny bottle of Molecule for her birthday the other week and didn't even bother to wrap it.

I won't drink tonight because it makes me talk too much and I start rabbiting. Anyway, I'm tired. It's been a tough day, of broken teeth and dislocated shoulders, basically all the usual stuff, plus a fifteen-year-old self-harmer and a toddler who'd swallowed an expensive camera battery. 'Will I still be able to use it once it reappears?' the dad asked. I felt like saying, 'Actually, sir, a lithium battery can burn through a child's oesophagus in under two hours, causing irreversible gastric damage and possible death, so let's just concentrate on getting the thing out, shall we?'

Christian's car is parked outside his parents' house. Good, that means Lydia's already here. He was picking her up after work and I was hoping he'd offer me a lift too, but apparently it wasn't convenient, which is fine, the walk will have done me good, and at least I'm not having to cook and I'm getting a free dinner.

I just hope it's not fish. I can't be doing with fish. Don't mind a breaded cod steak or a monkfish kebab, but I can't be doing with bones or eyes. What's all that about? Some scrap of fish lying on your plate with its burnt-out crusty eyeballs, trying to trick you into choking to death with any number of lethal needle-sharp bones lurking under the skin. Of course, the best remedy for removing a fishbone that's got trapped in your throat is to slather a small rolled-up piece of bread with peanut butter and swallow it down whole. With any luck the fishbone should stick to the peanut butter and travel safely down the gullet.

Choking is one of my biggest nightmares. I have used the Heimlich manoeuvre three times in my career, twice at home with toddlers and once at work. Lydia may be twenty-five years old but I still worry about her eating grapes. I can't help it, I see danger everywhere I look.

Nice enough house, thirties, very tidy front garden, very clipped hedge, but a slightly dead hanging basket by the porch, which is a bit depressing. I ring the doorbell and breathe in. I need to lose a stone because right now, if I'm not careful, I'm looking at type 2 diabetes before you can say Cornish pasty.

The door opens. A big man with a glass of red wine in his hand stands on the other side of it. He has the bulbous pitted nose of a man who likes a drink, and the whites of his eyes are a tiny bit jaundiced. His aftershave is strong and his shirt, which strains around the gut, is slightly yellow beneath the armpits. A sweaty, heavy drinker, then. But his voice is all booming confidence. 'Gaynor,' he bellows, 'come in.' A woman darts out of the kitchen behind him. She hops from foot to foot, a tea towel in her hand.

I recognise her immediately: she came into A&E three days ago with burns to her wrist and bruising to her arm. She said she fell over the cat and broke her fall by landing awkwardly on the hob. She'd been boiling milk and the ring was still hot.

I suspected she was lying then, now I know she was. There is no cat in this house. Lydia would have mentioned a cat, she loves them, even though they make her sneeze.

Christian's mother is wearing a lot of make-up. It is especially thick under her left eye. She flaps the tea towel and continues to jump about. If she were a child I would tell her to go to the lavatory, but she isn't a child, she is a middle-aged woman who has attempted to conceal a black eye with foundation and powder, and hidden the bruises on her arms under a long-sleeved blouse.

'I hope you like fish,' she says. 'Salmon,' she adds optimistically.

And that's when I smell it. Not just the fish, but something else. I smell a marriage gone wrong and a bullying dad and a son who just might take after his father in more ways than one. I smell all kinds of danger, but when I open my mouth, a voice that I recognise as mine merely says, 'Lovely.'

9

Anthea's Round Robin

Dear All,

*Apologies for the absence of a personalised Christmas
card (first time in twenty years!) but nonetheless
let me take this opportunity to wish you and yours
the compliments of the season and, in keeping with
time-honoured tradition, I enclose the annual edition of
Anthea's famous festive round robin – ta-da.*

With love,

Anthea Henderson

An auspicious start to 2016 saw the Henderson family
very much looking forward to a full twelve months of
fun-packed family celebrations, what with Roger due to

turn sixty in May; Nadine's forthcoming nuptials to her investment banker fiancé, Gideon De Beers, in June; and Max's much-anticipated and Cambridge-dependent A-level results hopefully providing the icing on the cake in August! Because, fingers crossed, once those three A-star grades were safely in the bag he would be off to the dreaming spires, and for the first time since our son was five, Roger and I would no longer be forking out for private tuition.

With this in mind, I had plans drawn up for a new kitchen extension, because let's face it, what woman in her right mind doesn't dream of a laundry room-cum-larder-stroke-boot room and pickling kitchen? As you can imagine, I already had a bulging file of chutney and preserve recipes gleaned from all over the world, including a traditional Hawaiian papaya and red plum jam with ginger that I was very much looking forward to bottling up.

So who could blame a girl for being giddy with excitement as the bells chimed in the brand-new year? But sadly, as Roger popped our celebratory bottle of New Year prosecco (a Christmas gift gratefully received from Cousin Steve and Aunty Beryl), the cork hit me in the eye and I spent the first few hours of 2016 down at A&E, making sure no permanent damage had been done to my left retina.

As luck would have it, I escaped the incident with my sight intact and the bruising went down in no time at all – thanks, I'm sure, to the application of a large organic fillet steak to the affected area, a meaty treat our fifteen-year-old Lab Buttons enjoyed immensely in his teatime doggy bowl, which was a relief, as he'd been off his food over Christmas. I remember saying to Roger, 'Someone's appetite isn't what it used to be,' and he said, 'Well it's not yours, porker. There's not a single liqueur chocolate left in this box.'

When I remonstrated, Roger pointed out that it wasn't Buttons who'd had to take three pairs of trousers down to the dry cleaners to have their zips replaced.

Which I thought was a bit below the belt, considering that the festive season is a very trying time for the emotional over-eater, and I was so upset I locked myself in the garage and ate a family-sized tiramisu.

Good job Nadine's fiancé Gideon De Beers had gifted Nadine and me a twelve-week intensive yogalates course for Christmas. Which was very thoughtful of him, even though Nadine cried because what she'd really wanted was a nice leather handbag she'd seen in John Lewis, and there was quite a prolonged frosty silence as a result.

No matter, by the end of February Nadine was back on speaking terms with Gideon and she and I were thoroughly enjoying our Wednesday yogalates mornings, especially once we got into the habit of celebrating our efforts in a certain little patisserie round the corner from the gym. So much so that when Nadine ordered her wedding cake from the establishment, they gave us a hefty discount for being such loyal customers. Sadly this saving was soon swallowed up by other wedding costs, including extensive alterations to the bridal gown in order to allow Nadine to physically move her ribcage on the big day.

March saw the family forgoing any Easter break so that Max could concentrate on his A-level studies, and to maximise revision efficiency we erected a camp bed for Max's personal tutor, a recently graduated rowing blue, in Max's bedroom, so that cramming could start bright and early and finish in the wee small hours. And judging by the amount of giggling we could hear across the landing, this was an arrangement that both lads seemed to thoroughly enjoy.

'Do you think they're having too much fun?' Roger asked, which was ridiculous, because as all mothers know, boys learn best through play. Although I must admit the bedroom did smell rather ripe by the end of the holidays, and I ended up plugging a Glade Bali sandalwood and jasmine air freshener into every socket in the room.

Sadly, after the holidays the tutor agency saw fit to swap Max's tutor for a much older, married father of three, who would on no account consider the sleepover option. Regretfully, as a direct consequence Max's enthusiasm for his subjects diminished and he became quite pale and lethargic. In fact, I was worried sick that he might have glandular fever, but when I took him to the doctor's his GP said, no, it wasn't glandular fever but neither was it anything that a course of antibiotics couldn't clear up in no time at all.

So that was a relief.

With Max back on form we were all very much looking forward to Roger's sixtieth-birthday hoedown and hog roast on the May bank holiday weekend. A joyful occasion some-what tempered by Roger's untimely bombshell that he had decided to retire in order to spend more time with his model train set and alpine village in the attic, and that from this day forth he wasn't setting foot in that sodding office again. He then ceremonially burnt every single one of his work ties (all of which I'd bought him as gifts over the years). A gesture, I felt, which smacked of showing off.

'Yes, but what would you know, Anthea?' joked Roger. 'You've never worked a day in your idle life.' And we all had a good laugh at that, because it was obviously a ludicrous thing to say when the fruits of my labour, including a particularly fine celeriac rémoulade, were spread out over the buffet table for all to see.

But what with the combination of the laughing, the acrid burnt-tie smell and the Pimm's which we had allowed Max to mix, I have to admit to being a teeny bit sick behind the car port and retiring to bed around 5 p.m. – but apparently it was a really marvellous party and the last time I got up to vomit, around 1 a.m., they were all still singing in the garden, so that was fun.

Sadly, due to Roger's sudden retirement shocker, we decided to put the kitchen extension on hold. I have to admit to feelings of bitterness and resentment, but once I took up Wednesday-morning calligraphy lessons at the local community centre I felt a great deal better. My GP also gave me some teeny little yellow pills, which was useful, considering that planning a wedding for one's only daughter can be quite a stressful business. But at least I was able to put my calligraphy skills to good use and I am proud to say that I created two hundred and fifty individual place names for the wedding-breakfast tables.

I've still got them somewhere, because Nadine and Gideon

decided to go in another, more contemporary direction, and I overheard Gideon asking Nadine if perhaps it was the menopause that made me so bonkers. But even so, on a somewhat overcast and chilly June day, the 15th, to be precise, we warmly welcomed Gideon into the bosom of our family, which I hoped made up for the fact that his own parents saw fit not to come as they were so disappointed in their son's decision to throw himself away on some dumpy girl from the wrong side of Colliers Wood.

Not being the type to bear grudges, we sent them a commemorative wedding album, self-published by Roger using the latest in computer software and a great many swear words. The end result was quite professional, even if Nadine did look like she could have been in the family way in some of the photos, and Gideon's name was misspelt on the cover.

All in all it was a most enjoyable day, marred only by the wedding cake being a tad sawdusty and Max going AWOL for several hours. We eventually discovered him fast asleep in the back of the wedding limo, although where his trousers disappeared to remains a mystery to this day.

Poor Max, it wasn't an easy summer for him, what with his father suddenly deciding that we could survive on his shoestring pension and that if Max wanted driving lessons then he could bloody well get a job and pay for them himself, which I thought was a bit much when I knew for a fact Roger had spent well over five hundred pounds installing a fully operational scale model of a ski lift above his alpine village.

I said to him, 'Those models of yours have more fun than we do. It's not like we've ever been skiing, and I've always fancied Switzerland,' to which he replied, 'So do I, only not with you.' Sometimes Roger's jokes can be a bit mean, and I may have accidentally crushed a miniature pine-effect ski chalet under the heel of my court shoe.

So, even though I thought he should concentrate on his studies, the ever-resourceful Max got a part-time job to pay for his driving lessons. He started work in a clothes shop called Abercrombie and Fitch, which I presumed was some nice gentlemen's outfitters down Regent Street. Sadly, when I popped in to deliver Max's forgotten packed lunch, I found the place to be a cross between the black hole of Calcutta and a den of iniquity. It was very dark and the music was very loud, and there were lots of girls with their bra straps and tummy buttons showing.

When I got home – after a restorative cup of chamomile tea in John Lewis – I phoned Messrs Abercrombie and Fitch to inform them that my son wouldn't be coming in again, and I assured Max he would thank me for it in the long run. To which he replied that hell would have to freeze over first, which I hoped might be a Shakespearian quote and a sign that he was actually knuckling down rather than just standing in front of the mirror and playing with his fringe.

Sadly, his results in August very much reflected that the styling of the fringe had indeed taken priority over his revision, and Max's predicted A-stars dissolved into a depressing array of Bs and Ds. In desperation, we decided to have his chemistry paper re-marked – a decision that not only cost us money, but the demotion of a B grade to a C and, with that, any dreams of dreaming spires crashed around our ears.

I doubt very much whether I shall set foot in Cambridge ever again, not even for the Christmas market, because ... one glass of Glühwein and I couldn't trust myself not to spit in the face of any student who did get in.

So, rather than embark on university life, Max has embarked on board a cruise ship as a junior entertainment officer and by all accounts, by which I mean his Facebook account (which I have managed to hack into under the pseudonym Gary the Abs), he is having quite the time of it.

Married life seems to suit Nadine, but unfortunately not her husband Gideon, who has moved back in with his parents to think things through. Sadly this is not just a reflection of the parlous state of their marriage, but also a condition of his bail, as there have been accusations of fraud at the bank where he works.

Nadine assures us that Gideon is innocent and that their marriage will survive this temporary blip. In fact, she seemed in quite high spirits as she showed Roger and me around their sumptuous penthouse apartment, with roof terrace, city views and underground car park complete with brand-new Lotus Elan!

As I said to Roger as he drove us home, 'Honestly, all I ever wanted was a kitchen-cum-pickling booth-stroke-calligraphy studio, and there's Nadine, only been married two minutes and she's already got a teriyaki plate and an estranged husband that doesn't get under her feet all day, using up the toilet paper and helping himself to perishables from the fridge.'

Roger, for some reason, took this as an excuse to move into the attic and exist on takeaway pizzas. He also said he'd never liked my soup, and that my cream of Jerusalem artichoke tasted like boiled vests.

I have to say that rankled, and as soon as he left the house I went straight to the attic and destroyed a papier-mâché Matterhorn with my bare hands.

From then on, I'm afraid, it was war, and the last time Roger and I exchanged a civil word was on my birthday, when the dog died and together we dug a hole for him in the back garden.

As I took Buttons' basket and squeaky rubber toys to the tip, I thought, Well, there's nothing left really, is there? Thirty years of married life and what have we got to show for it? Not a pickling kitchen, that's for sure.

All that's left is a dead dog buried under a barren pear tree, a couple of empty bedrooms covered in Blu-Tack scars and an attic full of model-train paraphernalia.

And I decided that as soon as I got home I was going to ask Roger to leave. Only by the time I got home he'd already gone, so I sat in the attic and I pressed a few buttons and watched a train go round in circles.

Then I operated the cable car over a rather realistic-looking glacier, and re-positioned some tiny model skiers, no bigger than my thumbnail. I perched some on the ski lift and some on the fake snow-covered slopes, and then I moved a small herd of scale-sized ibex with teeny-tiny hooves and miniature horns down to a moss-covered rocky outcrop, and I stayed up there, humming Christmas carols, until the night sky fell dark purple across the Velux window and the lights came on in all the little fake-pine chalets.

Happy Christmas, everyone, and may your new year be full of surprises.

10

Fifteen Minutes to Landing

My husband is holding my hand. This is because we are experiencing turbulence and he doesn't like it. I'm not fussed, I'm used to turbulence. It's been that kind of marriage.

The drinks trolley is rattling ominously and a female flight attendant – apparently they don't call them air hostesses any more – makes an announcement.

'Ladies and gentleman, due to adverse weather conditions, could you please return to your seats, make sure your lap trays are safely stowed and your seat belts firmly fastened.'

My husband is trying not to whimper. Poor Michael, the things he lets himself in for. This time it's Venice, a three-night romantic break in a much more expensive hotel than the one we honeymooned in twenty-five years ago.

I should have known when, the morning after our nuptials,

as we ordered bellinis for breakfast, his sperm still fresh inside me, I noticed that my husband of twenty-four hours couldn't help winking at the waitress, a short little seventeen-year-old cross-eyed Gina Lollobrigida lookalike.

Adultery is second nature to Michael. Just as some people are left handed or have a tic in their eye, he is unfaithful, and when I find out, which I inevitably do, he seems more surprised by the revelation than I am.

He always looks so shocked, as if he half believes he must have an identical twin who keeps doing these things.

Over the quarter of a century that we have been married, there have been four major love affairs, a dozen dalliances and any number of one-night stands. These I can always spot by the humming. My husband hums after an easy leg-over: they cheer him up. Some men need the occasional round of golf; Michael needs a bit of extra-marital. He is the sort of man who is constantly looking for the opportunity of a knee-trembler in a lift.

I think it's a combination of being better-looking than average and just a tad shorter than he would like to be. Therefore, the more furious I am with him, the higher my heel. For example, when we go out for dinner tonight I shall be wearing a three-inch spike. I think both of us are hoping that by Sunday night I will be in something slightly less stabby.

It's part of his punishment: the heels, the meals, the leather goods. This bumpy flight is extra salt to his wounds. Poor Michael, he is staring at the aircraft wings, willing them not to fall off, barely daring to blink.

It's an unwritten rule that over this long weekend I will order the most expensive wine on the menu – a crisp, peachy Viognier (he prefers red) – and I shall insist on a half lobster starter at every opportunity.

Then there's the shopping. I intend to mooch around the handbag shops until my husband is half dead with boredom. Let's face it, there's not much in this trip for him. Certainly no sex. I am in bedtime cold-shoulder mode: face full of moisturiser and a good book, covers pulled over my chest, bedside lamp on until I feel like switching it off.

We shall not speak of his latest peccadillo. I'm not a picker of scabs, but I do enjoy a good sulk. I rather like perching on the moral high ground in my ridiculous heels, looking down at my foolish, slightly-too-short husband. The pinch of my shoes reminding me of what he has done and how much it hurts.

This time, the woman in question is young and pretty – so far so clichéd. She's a receptionist at Jackson Black's, a pseudo old-school gentlemen's hairdressers in St James's, all traditional wet shaves and something for the weekend, sir. This is meant to be ironic. Instead of mints, they keep a bowl of condoms on reception. Ha-ha. The female staff wear pink candy-stripe uniforms nipped in at the waist; there is something of the sweet shop about the place. My husband attends Black's for styling and grooming. There's quite a lot of Greek blood in Michael, which manifests itself in the form of a monobrow, a furry, greying caterpillar that he likes to have expertly tweezered. Michael is a businessman; the fisherman eyebrows of his ancestors are something that must be professionally dealt with.

Whoo, that was a big one! It's like the sky is littered with potholes and this plane has no suspension.

Anyway, the girl is in her twenties. I blame the recession: minimum-wage life can be very dull, all H&M leggings and Tupperware lunches. Then along comes Mr Moneybags. Smells nice, likes Japanese food – of course he does, they're the only restaurants where he can guarantee the waiters are shorter than he is.

Seriously, most of my husband's affairs start with sushi. He is very good with chopsticks.

I think that, as a younger man, he probably practised. Some men use guitars to serenade the ladies, my husband uses his prowess with two sticks of bamboo. It's one of his sophisticated man of the world tricks: knowing his nori from his nigiri – tick; the Breitling diver's watch – tick; the Paul Smith ties – tick.

His philandering tendencies are given away by the fact that he is on first-name terms with the woman who sells Frederic Malle perfume at Liberty's. When my husband is serious about one of his little girlfriends he chooses her a signature scent, and the trouble with very expensive scent is that it lingers.

As soon as Michael came home *literally* smelling of roses – tuberose with notes of coconut and musk, to be precise – I knew he was up to something. This perfume costs over two hundred pounds a bottle. It clings.

I myself wear Portrait of a Lady, more cinnamon and sandalwood with overtones of ennui than ripe young rose. On a bad day, despite spritzing myself liberally with my exclusive

Parisian perfume, I can still smell the fury on me, waves of disappointment mixed with something that smells a bit like regret.

Maybe I should leave him. But the trouble with Michael and me is that we actually get on rather well. Apart from playing around, he does very little that is annoying, compared to most of my friends' husbands. Oiks and pigs, or dried-up old sticks with ridiculous opinions about immigration and heartburn. It's just time he grew out of his hobby, infidelity is for younger men. Like skateboarding.

Anyway, the next clue was the scratches on his back. When I pointed out these abrasions he tried to fake eczema. He even bought tubes of emollient creams and bath products containing soya oil, talked vaguely of going to see a dermatologist and proceeded to scratch himself all over, as if to camouflage the tell-tale talon tracks with self-inflicted decoy wounds. Dear God, he is fifty-two.

At this point I could have confronted him, but I like to build a watertight case. I don't want to be making vague accusations, I want names, dates and preferably receipts.

Don't get me wrong, there's evidence and there's evidence, and what I really didn't want was underwear in the glove compartment. That's what I call overly forensic. When one is a woman approaching Spanx-wearing age, the last thing one needs, when reaching for a tin of travel sweets, is to be confronted by the wisps of lace and cavernous satin cups that constitutes one's rival's knickers and bras, but that's what I got. I thought the bra was rather tarty: one of those Debenhams diffusion ranges that look oh so designer from

99

a distance, but on closer inspection turn out to be rather cheap and nasty.

Have you heard of that saying, why go out for a kebab when you've got steak at home? Well, sometimes my husband fancies a kebab. He has a penchant for girls who like Coca-Cola with their spirits and stagger around with blister plasters on their heels. Just girls, bog-standard girls.

Quite often they aren't very pretty, not close up. The very beautiful ones wouldn't give him a second look. He's like a magpie, searching out slightly damaged goods: the one with the mole on her chin, the one with a lazy eye, the one who'd been to a bad cosmetic dentist and consequently looked like a ventriloquist's dummy. Girls with self-esteem issues tend to be easier quarry, quicker to chase into bed with raw fish and tissue-wrapped gifts from Liberty's.

My husband's receptionist girlfriend is called Florence Bridgewater. I am grateful not to have a job which requires wearing a badge with my name on, but it did mean that she was easily identified. She even had a gold F necklace around her neck, another of my husband's trademark gifts. I wonder how many letters of the alphabet he has bought over the years. He is a man with a method: sushi, initial necklace, perfume, suspicious mobile phone behaviour, careless mistake, denial, tears, promises and treats, yada, yada.

We don't have children, which is for the best. A lot of my friends are stuck with twenty-somethings, massive cuckoos in their parents' nest. I couldn't be doing with that; our nest is full of beige suede and glass-topped tables. I have a walk-in panelled wardrobe complete with bespoke

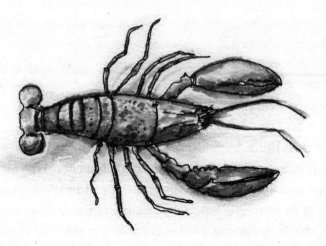

hand-turned shoe rack in polished walnut. Sometimes I sit on the floor inside my walk-in wardrobe with the doors shut and I breathe in the scent of wood and leather and I try not to cry.

A few people on this flight have been crying, white knuckles gripping armrests. Poor Michael, he's really sweating now, his airport-fresh Dan Brown unopened on his lap. He's in the aisle seat, keeping an eye on the cabin crew, and not just the pretty ones. I think altitude is the only thing that doesn't give my husband an erection. He is too nervous to notice that the Polish girl who served his double gin and tonic is the type that would normally have him licking his chopsticks and ordering a K for Katrine necklace online. Michael says, 'Once the air hostesses look worried, you're talking twin-engine failure.' Ours have returned to their seats while this little plane bucks like a donkey in the sky.

*

People tend not to scream in this kind of turbulence, but they do gasp. Dammit, I've splashed cava all over my linen trousers. Never mind, I can buy new trousers. That's if we actually make it to Venice. Michael is holding my hand so tightly now he must feel the sharp edges of my eternity ring digging into his palm. I think at this point he is regretting letting his Catholicism lapse; a rosary would give him something to do. I know my husband well enough to realise he will be blaming this on himself, *mea culpa* and all that. If he hadn't had the affair he wouldn't be in this situation. His wandering eye will be the death of him. God is angry.

Because for all my husband's urbane, businessman of the world veneer, deep down he is still a snivelling, superstitious boy. Right now he would like to be a child again, sitting on his fat Greek grandmother's lap, eating homemade baklava and not being bounced about in the sky, thirty thousand feet above the sea.

Finally the captain sees fit to reassure us from the cockpit.

'Ladies and gentlemen, this is your pilot, Captain James Barrington, just to say sorry that today's flight has been a bit Alton Towers. It's a bit stormy over the Med today, but we're through the worst and we'll have you safely down in no time.'

There's something in his voice: slightly amused, reassuring. The claustrophobic air of tension on board relaxes with an audible sigh of relief. The girl across the aisle, who has had her hoodie pulled over her head since we left Heathrow, manages to actually open her eyes and unclench her fists.

'Cabin crew to landing,' adds Captain Barrington.

My stomach lurches, but it's not just the drop in altitude.

We might be ten minutes from touchdown in Venice but I am no longer on this flight, I'm in a hotel bar in Manchester. Purple walls, dark purple carpet, every time I put my handbag down I lose it. In between scrabbling around on the floor for my handbag, I am spilling cocktails. The evening is sticky, five of us on a hen night. An afternoon of spa pampering, waxed and polished like Bentleys, we have done hot stones and facials; we are both relaxed and wired. My friend Amanda is getting married again – third time lucky, this time to a policeman, which is better than being married to a man who had four different mobile phones and kept rolls of bank notes in the bread bin. In the artificial light, we are well-dressed women in our forties; a smattering of Botox, a brace of fake breasts. We are oiled and exfoliated, pampered Prada-bag-carrying ladies. Close up, we are wrecked.

It's one of those hotels where footballers sometimes stay, corridors full of secrets, toilets steeped in tears. The bar staff are exhausted, hollow-eyed and bored of other people's excess. Air hostesses click across the marble foyer at midnight trundling cabin bags behind them, make-up cracking around their ears, smiles dropped en route.

It must have been around 1 a.m. when they joined us. We were at the screeching stage by then, but still good fun. It was Amanda who got them over, playing the hen card. They were still in uniform; the young one was gay, but the other one wasn't. Amanda tried his hat on – there is a photo on my phone, my soon-to-be-remarried mate wearing the peaked cap of our new best friend. The photo is as blurred as the night. Alcohol plays havoc with time and memory: when I next noticed my watch it was ten to three and I was struggling with my keycard. During the night I thought I heard rain and at 6 a.m. an alarm went off. It wasn't mine, mine plays the marimba. This sounded like an old-fashioned organ playing 'I Do Like to be Beside the Seaside'. I opened an eye and, lying beside me, not on the sand and not by the sea, was Captain James Barrington, and for the first time since I opened that glove compartment I laugh, and I laugh some more when I remember driving up to St James's and barging into Jackson Black's and throwing Florence's underwear into her gawping goldfish face, knocking the silly, twee dish of condoms flying, and storming out before a traffic warden had time to write me a ticket.

I laugh as the plane dips and sways through the clouds.

After all, what's sauce for the goose, ha-ha-ha.

Beside me, I realise my husband is silently weeping.

11

Mothers and Daughters

Unbelievably, Amanda has just texted to remind me where the casting is, and at what time. Well, how patronising can you get?

Honestly, it's like I'm some kind of imbecile. Mind you, I thought it was at half past not quarter to, so I can just sit here in the sun for a bit longer.

She took me out for a coffee last week. What kind of agent takes you out for a coffee? Vincent used to take me out for lunch: once a month, didn't flinch when I ordered the oysters. He had a lot of class, did Vincent.

Starbucks, if you please. Ghastly cardboard bucket of milky slop and a biscuit, one of those evil little nutty things that break your teeth. I didn't spend seven grand on a perfect set of gleaming veneers only to shatter them on a silly biscuit, or should I say biscotti.

I do rather a good Italian accent, even if I say so myself. I was the voice of a certain pasta sauce back in the eighties; paid for a new kitchen. I went full-on rustic farmhouse, complete with a terracotta-tile floor. Dreadful mistake – the noise every time you drop a fork! To be honest, it was a waste of money. I don't really need a kitchen, I only ever go in it to use the microwave. A shelf would do me.

Bossy girl, Amanda, enormous bottom. Seriously, the first time I met her and she walked out from behind the desk that used to be Vincent's, she just kept coming, like a car with a massive boot. I couldn't take my eyes off her, jeggings stretched to bursting point. She's got a pretty face, but she needs to get herself some contact lenses and learn how to use a pair of hair straighteners.

Funny how clever women can be so extraordinarily stupid about certain things. I may not have an A level to my name but give me a set of heated rollers and a tin of extra-strong hold and I'll sort you an up-do that could survive a nuclear blast.

My mum was a hairdresser; I've inherited the knack: accents and wigs are my speciality. I should have been a spy.

I've spent half my life touching up my roots. I went from mouse to red back in the seventies, softer than Cilla, bolder than Jane Asher. Changed my name from Carol to Coral. See – it all fits.

Amanda sometimes calls me Carol on the phone. My mum used to do that, but then she spent fifty years inhaling perm solution, which as we all know turns your brain to Swiss cheese. Anyway, Amanda's not my mum, she's only thirty-three and, the way I see it, if you're going to take 15 per cent then I think you should get your client's name right. To get her back, I call her Mandy.

Coral James, exotic but simple, the kind of name you might hear being announced on *This Is Your Life*: 'Ladies and gentlemen, will you please welcome Coral James.'

Can't tell you how many bits of blinking coral I've got. Every bloke I've ever been with thought he was doing something clever: birthdays, Christmas, coral necklaces, coral earrings. I don't even like coral; doesn't exactly sparkle, does it, just sits there, not knowing whether to be pink or orange.

I should have called myself Emerald or ... Diamond. I never got one of them and I really thought I would; I thought I'd meet some bloke who'd put a rock the size of a goose egg on my finger and I'd never have to worry again. I thought it would be all cruise ships and sailing the high seas, cocktails crossing the equator.

My fault. I had a whole string of fellas in my day, but I was picky, kept thinking the next one would be better-looking, more successful, then about fifteen years ago it was all men with eyebrows like owls, wearing short-sleeved shirts. I don't want to go out with blokes that look like they drive a minicab for a living. So I don't go out much, which is a shame because I do like dancing, but I've got no one to go dancing with.

All my girlfriends stopped being any fun years ago. They've all got fat arms and live in the country, lives revolving around slobbery black Labradors and tomato and courgette chutney, married to men with big red faces and breath like a badger's backside.

Even my gay friends have settled down. All the old backing dancers, the pretty boys and drag queens, all gone beardy and living with dachshunds in unfashionable places without Tube stations, South London mostly. I don't drive, and one's social circle tends to shrink when buses come into the equation.

At least this casting is in town, Soho, which is how it should be. Amanda wanted me to schlep out to Elstree a few weeks back for a bit part in *Holby*. I told her, 'I'm not flogging out to Hertfordshire in the hope of landing some daft part involving a woman who accidentally swallows a cocktail stick at a party.' Ridiculous! Apparently they asked if I could supply my own party frock. I said to Amanda, 'Do they want me to bring the canapés as well? I could do them a cheese and pineapple hedgehog.' She said, 'What's a cheese and pineapple hedgehog?' Television's not what it was, not that I've done any for a while. That's why Amanda thinks I should do this: she says it'll get me *seen*.

Apparently the writer's very up and coming. Twenty-six; she's won prizes. For swearing, I imagine. There's more effing and blinding in this play than there are full stops. It's called *Emily's Mother*, about a woman in her mid-fifties who feels guilty about her batty old mum. Well, we've all been there, haven't we?

Right, where am I going again? I did write the address on the back of an envelope but I seem to have left that at home. What did Amanda say in that text? Leicester Place. Might as well show willing. I never used to go to auditions – Vincent said I didn't have to – but Amanda said things are different

now. The climate's changed and I need to come down off my high horse.

I showed a lot of restraint at that moment. I laughed my famous wife-in-a-sitcom laugh, the one I used in *Meet the Ecclestones*. Remember that scene when the lemon soufflé I'd made collapsed in front of my husband's boss? *That* laugh. 'Haha-haha, Mandy,' I chortled, when what I really wanted to do was bite her face.

I've been to this address before. It's the Spotlight offices; they're on the third floor.

I don't take the lift, I like to keep in trim, and anyway I know an actress who was up for a part in a Hollywood movie, took the lift to the fifteenth floor, got stuck between twelve and thirteen, missed the audition, lost the part and by the time they got her out she'd soiled herself. Never really worked again – well, you wouldn't, would you, not once you've shat yourself in a Warner Brothers elevator. Last I heard, she was in telesales, poor cow.

I'm slightly out of puff by the time I reach the reception desk, but I take a deep breath and show my veneers.

'Hello, I'm Coral James. I'm here for the Emily casting.'

'OK, Carol, take a seat.'

Again the urge to bite is quite strong.

I've got the script with me. I'm not the best sight-reader in the world, obviously you don't have to know it inside out, but Amanda said I should try and get under the skin of the piece. I nearly said, 'Darling, I've been in this business forty-five years. When it comes to theatre, all I need to know is who's got the best dressing room, what time do we come down and how quickly can I get to Sheekey's?' All that crap about the art is such a lot of nonsense.

Can't really tell who's in for what. Of course there might be another casting going on, but I'd say the majority are in for the old mum – lots of porridge-coloured cardigans. Honestly, just because you're auditioning to play a woman who is losing her grip on reality, it doesn't mean to say you have to rifle Oxfam for inspiration. Not all old women dress like tramps. My mum was very smart. She was all clicks: click of her handbag, click of her powder compact, click of her heels, click,

click, clickety-click sixty-six. She loved a bit of bingo. A teeny bit common really, but you'd never guess, as long as she kept her trap shut. She was a smartly dressed woman with shiny black hair, but she gave herself away as soon as she opened her gob. Brummie, accent like a birthmark. I never had it because her hairdressing business did well and we moved to Solihull and I went to a nice girls' school, where my friends mistook my mother for the cleaner.

Well, look what the cat dragged in. I swear that's Lynette Shenley. I did radio with her years ago; she's gone very grey. I saw her in *Casualty* last year, incident with a flask of hot coffee, third-degree lap burns. Some people will do anything! I mean, we've all got bills to pay, but what price dignity? It's all very well the BBC warning folk about the dangers of opening boiling hot flasks of coffee whilst doing eighty in the fast lane of the M6, but there were some very graphic scenes concerning genital plastic surgery.

Course, I've had some. Not down there. Tiny little chin tuck about ten years ago, made it rather hard to swallow for a couple of months, lived on soup, lost twenty pounds, I'm delighted to say, so that was two birds killed with one large cheque to Harley Street.

Suddenly, a boy pops his head out from behind a door and calls for Miss Shenley.

Yup, correctamundo, that's Granny Shenley going in. They might even ask her to stay and read with me. Obviously I'd rather someone with a higher profile than a woman best known for burning her front bottom to play my mum, but

I don't think Julie Walters does Equity minimum, not in a room above a pub in Battersea. Yes a pub, and not on a Tube line, but as Amanda says, it's only two buses from mine, or a twenty-minute cycle should I so fancy. Silly bitch.

I miss my mum; that's why I'd like to play Emily. As Amanda, who has a degree in theatre studies from Warwick, would say, the writing resonates. God help me, I know what it's like to love your mum but not really want her in your life.

She was like a budgie, my mum, she'd witter on and I'd fantasise about throwing a tea towel over her head to shut her up. She'd get nervous and laugh too much and get hiccups. You can't have hiccups at an audience with Des O'Connor.

I didn't invite her down very often and I didn't go and visit very often either, and sometimes I didn't pick up the phone because I knew it would be her. I always thought there would be more time, but she died a couple of years ago on the number 41 bus. They only realised when it arrived back at the depot.

I was in Scarborough doing an Agatha Christie. Had to leave to sort out the funeral and everything, haven't really worked since.

The church was full, turned out a lot of people loved my mum. Bigger crowd than most matinee audiences: friends, old clients, neighbours, and they said so many nice things I got a bit upset and I got hiccups, which is very odd because I'm not the hiccupping type.

My mum did hairdos for nothing if people were skint or needed cheering up, which is probably why she had £249 in her bank account when she died.

I sold the shop and the flat above it, and I chucked all her china ornaments in the bin and paid off my mortgage. I thought I'd be quite nicely off, but things are a bit tight so I said to Amanda, 'I could do with some work, darling,' and she said, 'Would you consider advertising invisible hearing aids?' I said, 'I beg your pardon?' Cheeky cow.

Vincent lives in a retirement home for aged theatricals in Twickenham. I visited him last year and even though there was a framed photo of me arm in arm with Leslie Crowther on his bedside table, he thought I was a nurse, and I got upset because Vincent was my biggest fan and he hadn't got a clue who I was. When he fell asleep I sat and watched the blood slowing down in his veins and I couldn't even bring myself to hold his hand.

Oh, here she comes, Old Mother Shenley, she wasn't in long. Suddenly she glances over and gives me a look as if to say, 'Do I know you?' but I blank her because I can't be doing with all the what have you been up to and, well, I'm waiting to hear and who's your agent and fingers crossed and you never know. Because, let's face it, that woman is so washed up I'm surprised she doesn't leave a ruddy great tidemark against the wall as she leaves.

Then the boy pokes his head round the door again, looks at his clipboard, gives a vague look around the foyer and calls 'Ms James'.

I stand up and sort of cooee at him, which is ridiculous as the space between us is rather too small and somehow my handbag falls open and half a Pret sandwich falls out, which I pretend not to notice. Stepping carefully over bits of crayfish and rocket, I follow the boy into a small room, where a group of people are already gathered.

Two men, both wearing glasses, neither anything to write home about, and a woman, mid-fifties, possibly the producer, smiling in that relaxed way that women who have never had terrible teeth can. The fatter man, with the gold rimmed glasses, puts his hand out. 'Carol,' he bellows, 'good to see you,' and he indicates Mrs Smiley and says, let me introduce you to Elspeth, she's going to be our Emily, and Elspeth stands up and as she walks over to greet me she says, 'Hello, are you going to be my mummy?' Everyone laughs and I laugh too, but it's not a laugh I recognise, and as she offers me her cheek to kiss I bite her. Neatly on the earlobe, just a small pinch of a bite. Everyone is still laughing apart from Elspeth, and the second a look of alarm registers on her face it starts: I begin to hiccup. I hiccup and I hiccup and I hiccup and I hiccup all the way home.

12

Valerie Lashes Out

I have been sent to the stock room to calm down, an instruction guaranteed to have the opposite effect. I am bathed in sweat, teeth clenched, spitting swear words, hackles bristling. Mind you, my hackles seem to be in a constant state of bristle these days – due, no doubt, to the idiots that I must endure on a daily basis.

Call them visitors, call them customers, call them what you will. Under my breath I call them all kinds of names: fools, morons, time-wasters, filthy-handed grubs, gormless, barely functioning vertebrates, oafish plodders, thickos, tortoise brains and spud faces.

It has come to my attention that culture is wasted on the general public. Most of them are only here for the flapjack. Of course, even worse are the ones that bring their own flapjack and sit in the car park with their flasks and sandwiches, looking at the fountains periodically spitting brown water through the corroded appendage of a rusty flute-playing nymph. The freeloading numbskulls.

Smethwick House is a Grade 2 listed Victorian Gothic pile in Derbyshire. Obviously it cannot compete with the raging beauty of its show-off neighbour Chatsworth – we have neither film nor TV credits to our name; Judi Dench has not graced our terraces in a fetching period hat.

Neither do we have National Trust or English Heritage status. Possibly because there is a filthy great seventies kitchen extension round the back and some of the window frames are plastic. Nonetheless, Smethwick is an architecturally interesting small mansion house built by a nineteenth-century eccentric to house his collection of antiquities and collectables, some of which are still on display today. It's the usual mishmash of giant ostrich eggs and moth-eaten stuffed weasels in smoking jackets, wax flowers thick with dust, fertility masks, shrunken heads and fossils.

Of course, a great deal of the good stuff got burnt back in the last century, when Smethwick lost a wing after a somewhat debauched New Year's Eve party supposedly heralding a Happy New 1953. Its silhouette has never been the same since.

The place is run, on paper, by some faceless trust down in London, and in real life by us, the volunteers. Pensioners mostly, lots of widows, plus a sprinkling of divorcees and ancient spinsters, myself included, I am most grateful to say. Couples tend to avoid the volunteer rota. After all, they have better things to do with their time: coupley things, visits to see grandchildren, ballroom dancing, jumping on board cruise ships to stare at sunsets – or simply sitting on the sofa together, holding hands. The smug puke-makers, I call them.

They visit here and mostly compare it unfavourably to that other place we went to, remember? The one with the really marvellous cream tea.

Cream teas are not a highlight of the Smethwick House experience. Deirdre bakes cakes which taste of disappointment; it's almost a skill.

I'd like to see her in the *Bake-Off* tent; I'd like Mary Berry to lift one of Deirdre's cakes to her lips and say, 'What do you think, Paul? Is there not a residual flavour of ennui?'

The ingredients of Deidre's cakes may be the usual butter, flour, sugar and eggs, but they also contain bitter regret and a soupçon of what might have been.

The Dalgliesh family, who own the house, are still in residence. Well, Lady Dalgliesh occupies a small suite of rooms in the west wing. A red velvet rope droops across the bottom of a forbidden staircase, a sign reads 'Private try'. It should, of course, read 'Private No Entry', but some of the letters have worn away.

Lady Dalgliesh is ninety-three and mostly watches television from her bed. She is entirely deaf, so when one is on Main Hall duty, one can hear the hysteria of daytime television emanating from her quarters. Her favourite is *Loose Women*.

I have been serving Smethwick for over twenty years. The trouble with being a volunteer is that you haven't officially got a job, so you've nothing to retire from and anyway, this is the sort of thing retired people do, so I'm really not sure when I'm supposed to stop.

If I wasn't doing this I would have to occupy myself with hospital visits or meals on wheels. Pre-war middle-class women like me were brought up with a sense of duty, which is a terrible bind because if I didn't have this compulsion to do something, to be a valuable and useful member of society, to contribute to the community, I could just lounge around like Lady Dalgliesh.

The upper classes are so wonderful at doing whatever they please, be it slaughtering foxes, blowing birds out of the sky or simply lolling around watching rubbish at full blast on the television.

My father was in the clergy. I expect that had something to do with it, and my mother was a good Christian woman, who sat on a lot of committees and raised money for poor children in Africa, despite being a complete bitch at home.

There is no uniform at Smethwick, although we all tend to wear a variation on a theme. For the women it's plaid skirts, Shetland sweaters over a simple blouse, a brooch at the throat – cameos and Celtic designs are popular. Pearls tend to be single-stranded and real. One or two have pretensions of artiness and there are occasional sightings of purple suede boots with fringing, and embroidered waistcoats; what I call the Virginia Woolf mob. The male volunteers wear what old men tend to wear: navy sweaters, moleskin or cord trousers. Though of course we have our resident *colourful* character, with his ridiculous collection of bow ties, which I assume he would like us to comment on. 'Oh good morning, Nigel, I see it's spots today,' but we all studiously avoid mentioning them, just to annoy him.

All staff members are issued with a purple lanyard holding a plastic envelope with our name and the title GUIDE above the Smethwick coat of arms, which features a pair of crossed swords over a curly-horned ram.

Some people volunteer to make friends. I've watched them chum up, women old enough to know better giggling like schoolgirls, insisting on taking their tea breaks at the same time, grey heads together as they pore over each other's various crochet and cross-stitch projects.

Personally, I like to keep myself to myself. I bring a sandwich from home because I don't want one of Deirdre's ham and despair baps, and I like to find myself a nice quiet corner where I can settle down with a murder mystery.

I'm not the most anti-social: there's an old boy, goes by the name of Justin, who comes into the staff room, removes his hearing aid and puts it on the window sill, which I think is international sign language for leave me the hell alone, which would be fine if it wasn't such a disgusting insanitary article.

Ten of us: three upstairs, three down, two in the gift shop, two on the tickets desk at the entrance.

There's a lot of standing. Sitting is discouraged, which I think, considering most of us are over sixty-five, is a bit harsh, and consequently there's a lot of time off for varicose-vein ops.

The cushiest job is on entrance tickets, because that's officially a sitting-down position, but you have to be computer savvy, and a number of us are what one might call technophobes.

Sadly the men seem to be the more computer literate, because they've done courses in the local library, but they type like they've got hooves so they're unbearably slow, apart from Arthur, who used to work in intelligence and is therefore not only a dab hand with a Microsoft Excel spreadsheet but can type with both hands.

Arthur and I have a common interest in history, although he leans towards the military, whereas I have a more social bent.

He's a rather new addition to our ranks, is Arthur, and a cut above some of the other shuffling fools insomuch as he doesn't seem to have anything terribly wrong with him. Some of my male colleagues are a walking encyclopaedias of decrepitude, dandruff sprinkled like parmesan cheese over their jacket collars, toilet brushes in each nostril.

Of course, once upon a time, some of them had wives who made sure they didn't go out with gravy-stained ties. Sadly widowers with cataracts tend not to bear close inspection.

Arthur, on the other hand, has a stain-free crotch and I've never heard him do that annoying throat-clearing thing that is just one of the reasons why I refuse ever to share a shift with Bernard.

I keep checking the door, but bizarrely it seems they've locked me in from the outside; apparently disciplinary action may be taken. Well whoop-di-whoop, it's not as if they can sack me. I shall simply withdraw my services. To be honest, I'm sick of being treated like an unpaid skivvy, which is why I'm filling this carrier bag with a few choice items from the Smethwick House souvenir collection.

They'll miss me more than a few cheap tea towels, a selection of fridge magnets and some mouldy old Smethwick House Kendal mint cake.

You can call it thieving if you like, but I'm not the only one putting my filthy hands on things they shouldn't be touching.

I've got eyes like a hawk. Vigilant with the school parties, I can always spot the kid who can't be trusted near the plastic arrangement of Victorian victuals in the kitchen. Bright pink silicone leg of ham, fake grapes and an amusing rubber mouse nibbling at a pretend cheese! Really, sometimes I think we try too hard to entertain the school parties. Real life shouldn't have to resemble a cartoon to hold their interest.

'Oh Valerie, you're so strict,' says Heather. 'The kiddies only want to have fun, but I say there's a fine line between fun and vandalism. Teachers who issue children with biros to fill in their history worksheets on the premises should be made to stay behind and clean any subsequent graffiti off the walls.

They mostly try and hide their scribblings on the walls behind curtains, but I know where to look. It's not the language that upsets me, it's the spelling.

'How do you know the littlie in question doesn't have dyslexia?' asks Heather, making her big blue eyes go all round like marbles. 'She's right,' says Arthur, whose seven-year-old grandson apparently struggles with his reading. I said, 'Well, dyslexia or not, judging by the accompanying anatomically correct representation of a certain part of the male anatomy, whoever did it is no slouch in the biology department.'

'You're making Heather blush,' says Arthur, and it's true, because she's that kind of woman, the type who goes pink and giggles and touches her hair, the type whose china-blue eyes fill up with tears when faced with a story in the *Daily Mail* about some lout being cruel to a cat. She's the worst type of female pensioner, the type who keeps her travel pass in a pretty little embroidered case and visits 'the little girls' room' to 'powder her nose'.

She had her sights set on Arthur as soon as she arrived bearing a Tupperware of homemade fudge, sob story at the ready: how she'd moved up from the Midlands after her husband died to be closer to her daughter and her grandchildren, yak yak.

How she used to be very active in her local amateur operatic society and how her daughter thought volunteering at

Smethwick House might help her integrate with the local community.

She is sixty-seven, useless at cards, likes pastel shades, drives a silly little car and is vain about wearing her glasses, hence she's a liability just about anywhere. She approaches the computer as if it were a python about to strike at any moment. If only it were and it would.

'Oh Arthur, help me,' she whinnies and he trots over because Arthur likes to help, and he's a gentleman. Lord knows he's even helped me fix my bike on a number of occasions – this morning, for example. I came a cropper coming up the drive, and not only did he help me to my feet, he had the offending flat tyre in a washing-up bowl of warm water before you could say puncture. As soon as he saw where the bubbles were coming from, hey presto, he glued down the repair patch.

It's not as if I couldn't do it myself, but sometimes it's nice to let someone else take charge, especially when you've laddered your tights and your knees are bleeding quite badly.

'Ergh,' said Heather, whom Arthur had instructed to fetch the first-aid box, which is actually an old Diamond Jubilee Peek Freans biscuit tin containing an assortment of plasters, three paracetamol and an inhaler.

'I feel a bit queer,' she whimpered. 'It's the blood, you see,' and of course the next thing Arthur's making her sweet tea and supplying her with an emergency staff-room rich tea.

Left to my own devices, I dabbed at my knees with some paper towels, staunched the bleeding, applied a number of variously shaped plasters – one of which featured cartoon Smurfs – and then put the tyre back on the bike wheel myself.

As I came back indoors Heather said, 'You're so capable, no wonder you've never been married, Valerie. After all, you don't really need a man.' It was very subtle, but what she was implying was that I was enough of a man myself, and I will admit that at five foot eleven, with size-ten feet, it's hard to play the little woman. I've never really minded, but at that moment she made me feel like a female impostor, and then they laughed, both of them, Arthur and Heather.

As I walked up the stairs to take up my position in the portrait gallery I felt the heat crawl around my neck. A slow burn, darker than the girlish pink that Heather manages to summon up every time someone drops something vulgar into the conversation.

Indeed, a glance in the age-spotted mirror at top of the stairs revealed my blush to be a feverish, bloodied hue that licked dangerously around my collarbone and I watched myself carefully pick up a large ginger jar from the oak trestle table on the landing and turn to drop it over the banister.

I caught him on his high, intelligent forehead and he slumped forward, uttering the coarsest of language, but it didn't seem to bother her. Neither did the swearing, nor the blood, quite a lot of blood, all over the Chinese rug.

It didn't take long for everyone to come running, or rather shuffling and limping. 'Call the ambulance!' shouted Heather. 'And the police!'

And that's why I have been put in here whilst the authorities decide what to do with me, and that's why I am taking all these souvenirs. After all, the sirens are very close now and I doubt very much I shall ever be coming back.

13

Lorna's Holiday

This is a very smart hotel. I'm choosy about certain things: the thread count of my sheets; the quality of my morning pastries; complimentary towelling robe and slippers; the end of the lavatory roll folded as carefully as if it were an invitation from the palace; and no children – that's very important. I don't really like them, all that shrieking and showing off.

I am here for peace and quiet. I am recuperating: I have had an operation. I need to rest, recover my strength and, more importantly, my vocal cords. Silence is golden in more ways than one.

I rather like being on doctor's orders; it has given me licence to spend a lot of money. Of course, I could have recuperated in a Ramada Inn, but where's the fun in that?

Views are important. 'Dubrovnik's stunning coastline',

promised the brochure, and it is quite pretty. Nothing out of the ordinary, though. Sometimes, when I'm bored, I'd like to see a volcano smoking in the distance, a forest fire, something to give the place a bit of edge. But it's what you'd expect: grey rock and blue sea, the sun a yellow ball in a sky that occasionally clouds over.

The other guests hate that. The atmosphere changes. Oiled-up sun worshippers, squinting at the sky; they can order as many mojitos as they like, but they cannot demand the pool boy drag the sun from behind those clouds. Stupid sun, acting up like a shy child, peeping out for a minute and then disappearing behind its mother's grey skirts again. One can hear the tutting.

I'm not fussed, I've been here two weeks and my tan matches my suitcase. I simply sit and people-watch from behind my oversized Versace glasses. No one is particularly interested in me, because I am a fat middle-aged woman.

That I am rich is a given: there is no riff-raff here. I have the requisite number of diamond rings; third finger right hand mostly (I am not married). My handbag displays the giveaway crossed Cs of Chanel, and it is large. After all, any penny-pinching PA can have a *small* Chanel handbag, but I find size does matter. This handbag cost four thousand pounds and most people here will know that. The devil is in the detail: my kaftan might be a size eighteen, but it's an Emilio Pucci from Harrods.

Here, one is judged by appearance. Of course, if you are young and thin and good-looking one automatically gains extra points. The blonde girl who wraps herself like seaweed around her John F. Kennedy-lookalike fiancé is a top-scoring type, but there is a hint of desperation around her melon-only meals, her frantic yoga moves. He is altogether more impressive, jaunty parrot-print shorts which smack both of designer and of devil may care. Occasionally his eyes slide over to the red-haired American heiress who must be twenty-three and doing Europe with Mommy and the man I can't believe is Daddy, a short, cigar-smoking toad of a man.

A pair of older Italian sisters are interesting. One is petite, the other a sort of giant version. They wear similar outfits in entirely different sizes; the big one has feet like canoes. They smoke and laugh a lot, I imagine they could be rather fun if one could be bothered. The English are by far the dullest: dimple-thighed women wishing they'd dieted earlier in the year, obsessively covering themselves up with their sarongs, their balding husbands reeking of having recently retired. These are the ones one must avoid making eye contact with. Their children are at university and they will bore you for hours about Charlotte or Phoebe or Zack and how they worry. Like I care.

I keep myself to myself. A wide-brimmed hat is useful, and if it all gets too much I take myself back to my room. I'm paying a fortune for this suite – I might as well spend some time in it. I'm on a corner with a balcony that wraps itself around the outer edge of the hotel; from the front I can see the lights of Dubrovnik and from the side I can see across a narrow inlet to a large white bougainvillea-clad villa perched on the cliff. Slightly too close for comfort, it's obviously available for private rental and currently it's occupied by what seems like two British families – both, unfortunately with a brood of children. About five of the little blighters: two boys of around thirteen, a couple of eleven- or twelve-year-old girls and a tiny one. A mix of dark heads that swim like otters in the water directly beneath my balcony and three pork-sausage-limbed blonds who are forever having to be creamed up by their Boden-catalogue mother.

The mothers are extraordinary. They seem to have come on holiday to shout, issuing orders at the tops of their voices like sergeant-majors in drag. Their children have inter-changeable London prep school names, Saskia and Hamish, Emily, Ollie and Cicely; the fathers are all navy polo shirts and back-slappingly competitive but jolly good sports. 'Play fair and share,' they bellow at their children whilst the mothers shriek about lunch and being careful and not being silly and stop it.

Sometimes before I go down for dinner, when I am resting on my bed, being absolutely silent as I have been advised, I can smell their barbecue supper wafting in through my bedroom window on the evening breeze. They eat at about six thirty – I suppose the small ones get tired. At half past eight I go down for my dinner and by the time I get back to my room the lights across the bay are dimmed and all I can hear is the occasional burst of laughter, the clink of glasses, bottles being thrown into a bin. Parenthood seems to drive most people to drink.

From what I can gather, children aren't as happy as they're meant to be. There's a lot of crying and jealousy and he said, she said and no I never involved, and as I watch the permutations of other people's families I'm again relieved to be the only child of long-dead parents. There is only me to worry about, just me and I'm fine. Well, I will be, I had the very best man in the business. Anyone who is anyone in music goes to Mr Roberts, he's a miracle worker so they say. I just have to take extreme care at this stage of my recovery.

I must admit, the food here is very good, which is a relief because I can't really be bothered to go into town, weaving my way through back alleys with a guidebook in one hand and Google Maps in the other, trying to find some dingy little place that does the most authentic sardines. Who wants authentic sardines? Peasant food, full of bones. Here at the hotel the menu is a great deal more lobster than sardine. There's a tank in the dining room. Lobsters are intriguing; they are also delicious and the chef is a dab hand with a classic thermidor.

I eat what I like: one of the perks to my job is no one expects me to be thin, although when I am working I have to avoid dairy. Here on my holiday/convalescence, food is an enormous source of comfort. Meals are the highlight of my day. There's not much else for me to enjoy: I don't like swimming, and I'm too fat for walking around the city walls, crawling over ramparts and all that kind of nonsense.

I've been here long enough to have developed a routine. Before breakfast I make myself a cup of Earl Grey tea and take it out onto the balcony. I attempt some of the exercises the surgeon gave me, and although I've been told it's perfectly safe I'm terrified of the consequences of pushing myself too hard. Mind over matter, Mr Roberts says.

At about 9 a.m. the children from the villa opposite start bouncing down the steps cut into the rocks to their swimming jetty. Golden sands are not this region's speciality, but there is a perfectly serviceable wooden platform with a set of metal steps into the sea. It's safe enough.

One of the boys, the dark-haired lad, has taken to jumping off a rocky promontory halfway down the cliffside. It must be a leap of about five metres. The first time he did it his father pretended to be cross: 'You should have asked me first, Ollie, but good jump, son. Well done.'

The boy is thrilled by his bravery; he struts like a bantam. 'Quickest way in,' he tells the others, and he does it again, leaping and beating his skinny chest and making Tarzan noises. Then his apple-pip-headed sister does it and everyone claps. Two in, three to go.

'Come on, Hamish, jump!' shouts the blond children's father. 'You're the eldest, don't be a wuss.'

Unfortunately Hamish is one of life's natural wusses. Hamish swims in his T-shirt because he is embarrassed about his puppy fat; he wears glasses that he gets panicky about misplacing. He is a solid, pink boy who is always the first to ask when lunch is. When Hamish says he's starving the other children make pig-honking noises and his father snaps, 'You can't possibly be starving, you've just had your breakfast.' But I understand how Hamish feels.

The continental bread basket and pastries are very good here at the hotel – I don't have cooked every day, and so far I have resisted the whites-only omelette. I imagine it must be like eating a cloud.

My laughing Italian sisters have the messiest breakfast table. There isn't a single thing they won't use as an ashtray: orange peel, brioche, empty boiled-egg shells. I'm not sure if people notice me or not. If so, they will conclude that I'm very anti-social. I don't even speak to the waiters, I just point to what I want in the menu. They probably think I'm rude.

The people in the villa usually go out from about midday. It's certainly very quiet between the hours of twelve and four. They leave their towels and fishing nets scattered about on the jetty, a plethora of lilos and inflatable dinghies. No doubt the parents want them to experience some local culture, put their fingers into the battle scars of the old city, eat some bony sardines, just like the fishermen, blah, blah, blah.

They usually return when I am napping in the afternoon. I find their squabbling quite comforting, and there is a great deal of rock-jumping. The older girls do it holding hands and screaming, which is a bit much. Only Hamish and the tiny girl are yet to jump; the tiny girl is told she is too small and reacts by throwing her small plastic Croc shoe at her father's head. She's a bit of a madam, that one, and personally I don't think a smacked bottom would go amiss. 'How about you, Hamish?' shouts the man who isn't Hamish's father. 'He doesn't have to,' argues Hamish's sister, but the dark-haired boy who is forever looking for new rocks to jump off flaps his elbows and makes a chicken noise. Poor Hamish, at least it makes a change from being oinked at. He should laugh it off but he can't: his face goes scarlet and he waddles back to the villa in a huff. 'Is Hamish crying?' asks the tiny girl. 'Oh for Christ's sake, Hamish, do you always have to be so unutterably wet?' shouts his father, sounding genuinely pissed off.

I am flying home today. The sky is gunmetal grey; I felt the change yesterday. It's good to be leaving, the poor weather will make everyone peevish, and anyway, I've had every single thing on the lunch menu and there is an invasion of flying ants, so good riddance really.

Everything is packed, including the medication I've got left and I try to feel calm about the future. There is no reason why I shouldn't make a full recovery. After all, I have been a textbook patient. I must have confidence. I make myself a cup of tea and mooch out onto my balcony. Dubrovnik looks diminished and blurred today: none of the pleasure boats are out, the waves splash further up the rocks than normal, the day feels darker. I almost check to see if I'm wearing sunglasses but I'm not, there's no need.

Across the inlet I see Hamish walking down the cliff path. He looks as if he's dressed for going home too, trainers and a shirt. Down on the jetty he retrieves a tethered rubber dinghy from the water that slaps menacingly around the jetty. He pulls at the stopper with his teeth and sits on the thing, his generous backside squeezing all the air out of the inflatable, and then he makes his way back up the steps.

Halfway up, he stops, drops the dinghy and walks over to the rock he has never managed to jump off. Suddenly he pulls off his clothes. Tugging angrily at his too-tight shirt, ripping down his chinos, he strips himself of everything save his boxer shorts. He stands on the rock and looks down, removes his glasses and then, before he can change his mind, walks off the cliff. He doesn't jump. You have to jump, you have to clear the rock face, you can't just drop off the thing. I hear his head on the rock, a knock like room service; I see his glasses where he left them; I hear the splash, but I don't see him surface. I keep waiting to see his pink, triumphant face; I wait to hear him shout. I want him to yell 'I did it!' but there is nothing, and in the second before I do anything I think about my career and my voice and the operation and my fear that I will never be as good as I was and how opera has been my life and how I have been told to rest and so I haven't spoken for a fortnight because I have been too frightened to even try. I have pointed at waiters I have turned away from eye contact, I have treated my vocal cords like spun sugar, but I have to do something, and I open my mouth and I start shouting.

'Help! Help the boy!' My voice is clear as a ship's bell, and I shout, I shout – as loud as any mother – for the boy's life.

133

14

George's Cake

I am a dab hand with a Victoria sponge. The trick is to add a little cornflour to the mix, gives it a lighter, airier quality. This cake is textbook: golden brown, springy to the touch, smelling of celebration.

I don't just do cakes. I can turn my hand to anything in the kitchen, from lonely little mushroom omelettes for one to the full-on Christmas dinner fandango. Over the years I have learnt how to bone a chicken, dress a pheasant and peel an onion without crying. You hold it under cold running water.

When I first married my husband thirty years ago my culinary repertoire consisted of three things with mince and any type of fruit crumble that you care to mention, including tinned. These days I can make pastry in my sleep,

I never look at a stale crust without thinking what I could use the breadcrumbs for, and it's been years since I've curdled a mayonnaise.

I'm a natural. Some people have green fingers, I have cooking hands, burnt fingers and extra-strong wrists from juggling heavy pans. I am a very well-equipped woman, but I deserve to be. I may not have paid for this kitchen out of my own pocket, but I have paid in kind.

It's ten years since George decided we should refurbish the kitchen. He spent a lot of money: it's made to measure. As George said, 'None of your cheap rubbish.' He didn't like the men who installed it, made me buy a supermarket own-brand jar of coffee for the labourers: 'They won't know the difference, Bea.' But they did, because one of them turned up with his own ground beans and a cafetière.

It's traditional – George doesn't like anything modern. I went for solid oak units, it was every woman's dream kitchen at the time, Shaker-style, with pans hanging from the ceiling, copper-bottomed, heavy enough to knock out an intruder. We have French windows and I used to lie awake wondering if someone was breaking in. I take sleeping pills now and browse the Lakeland catalogue until the darkness comes.

In some respects this kitchen was my reward for learning to cook, for becoming a dab hand, a credit. Over the years I have spent a lot of time in here. George has got his money's worth. My husband and I may not have had sex for many years but I cook him a hot breakfast every morning, and in this department at least I am adventurous and experimental. Last week I devilled him some kidneys. My husband is a gourmand; he has a fine palate and the waistband to prove it. George is quite fat. He does a lot of entertaining, he has clients, interchangeable business types in suits, their various wives ranging from the subdued to the exuberant. The only ones I can't be doing with are the ones with allergies or no appetite. My job is not to entertain but to impress the only way I know how, not with my sparkling wit or conversation – because as George says, 'When you don't know what you're talking about it's best you try to look pleasant and shut up' – but with my cooking tricks, my conjuring of en croutes and soufflés, my patisserie skills and the way I can spin molten sugar into complex golden webs.

George is keen on presentation. Woe betide a drippy gravy boat. He gets this from his mother, an exacting woman whom I fed every Sunday on the dot of 1 p.m. for almost three decades. She died last year, bolt upright in a wing chair with her cameo brooch at her throat, but George still expects a roast with all the trimmings. He likes the silver well-polished; he likes to stand at the head of the table and sharpen the carving knife in his Sunday best, napkins starched, whilst I sit and wonder why he is wearing a tie.

The cake is cool to the touch now. I can begin to decorate it very soon. I have an entire cupboard dedicated to the art of food ornamentation, piping bags and nozzles of all description, twenty-six of them in a special case like a set of screwdriver heads. I am as equipped as any surgeon with my silicone moulds and edible golden stars.

George is sixty tomorrow and I am rolling out lemon fondant icing. He has a very sweet tooth, which is why I have made him a pudding every day of our married life. Sometimes it's been something simple, a pear poached in red wine. My friend Philippa was flabbergasted: she just chucks her husband Ian a Ski yoghurt, says he's lucky to have a choice between rhubarb and raspberry. The only time George hasn't had his pudding is when I've been in hospital. Over the years my crème brulée has been the outstanding favourite, but he is also a big fan of the pavlova – heat the sugar, that's what you've got to do with meringues.

I would have liked children, but it didn't happen. Maybe that's why I've felt I had to make it up to George in other ways: the soldiers I cut for him; the sweet, sticky glaze on his homemade brioche; the scratches on my arms from picking blackberries for his jam; my grated knuckles; my blistered, straight from the oven tasting tongue; my burnt and sliced fingertips. I'm sorry, I'm sorry, I'm sorry.

We have never spoken of blame; we never went down the route of tests and intervention. His mother was convinced it was my fault, she had three sons and they each had children apart from poor George. What a shame, he had so much to offer. And I felt like screaming 'What about me? I have so much to offer too. Imagine the birthday cakes that I could create, imagine the contents of their nutritionally balanced lunch boxes.' But I didn't say anything. I swallowed hard and fed her every Sunday, the only daughter-in-law (as far as I'm aware) who ever did, all those roasts, chicken, beef, lamb – she didn't like pork, it repeated on her – all those crispy on the outside but fluffy in the middle roast potatoes. 'Just one dear, I'm watching my weight.' Another dig at me, red-faced from the kitchen, skirts straining at my podgy waist. No matter that her son was positively fat.

In my imagination my children are coated in homemade-biscuit crumbs; they are round-tummied ghosts. I would have liked three, but I'd have made do with one.

Lenny came in to my life a year ago. What can I say? I was fat and lonely and he's a cocker spaniel. Who'd have thought a dog could look so pleased to see you? George wasn't keen: 'We've never had to bother with anything like that before,' he said. But I promised not to involve him, I promised not to get one that barked or chewed things. Well, obviously he does, but it's my shoes and slippers that Lenny seems to like. He's a very clever dog, he leaves George's things alone. It's as if he knows.

As soon as George arrives home Lenny quietens down. He goes into obedient mode; sometimes I catch his eye and I feel like laughing out loud. Lenny is not by nature either quiet or sensible, he's a glorious, lovable hound. Everyone knows him, he is the clown prince dog of the park, 'Here comes Lenny'. People are pleased to see him, he is my passport to popularity. Most of the people that I see in the park don't know me by my own name, they know me because of Lenny.

He says he can smell him. George has started making me hold my hands out for him to sniff when he comes home from work. He says he doesn't want doggy smells in with his food.

I wash my hands under scalding water, I slather them with a heavily rose-scented hand cream. Weirdly enough, most days my hands smell of garlic-scented roses.

Right, where's my thingy – the doo-dah – because before I roll the icing out over the cake I need to slice it through horizontally, to make two halves of the sandwich. I have a special tool, an adjustable cake wire, which is somewhere under here. Ah, here we are. It has a stainless-steel blade, not the sort of thing a woman can carry around in public. There is something of the offensive weapon about it, but see how easily the cake is garroted.

Now I just need to fill the middle with jam and whipped cream, put something sticky on the top to glue down the fondant icing and then I'll add some special finishing touches. After all, sixty is quite a landmark birthday. I want to give George something he'll remember for ever.

I used to whip cream by hand, but since Lenny arrived I've started making use of a lot more kitchen gizmos and gadgets. As Liz says, 'You're not George's slave, Bea, you don't have to be a prisoner in your own kitchen.' She's got a Labradoodle, they're quite silly dogs. Lenny is a great deal more intelligent than Lulu but they're still great friends, like me and Liz. She doesn't have children either, so I don't have to put up with all those interminable conversations about GCSEs and UCAS forms. I don't think most parents have any idea quite how dull they and their dreary offspring are. Liz's very well travelled, but she doesn't know one end of a packet of filo pastry from the other.

OK, homemade strawberry jam, very easy. The most important thing is to make sure your jars are sterilised, otherwise it doesn't matter how high your pectin content, there's going to be mould.

There we go, lovely bright red jam. Spread that nice and thick over the top of the bottom half. Then see, I'm loading the whipped cream on top. I'm using a flexible silicone spatula to take the cream from the bowl, no licking. I've lost a bit of weight recently. If I want to nibble then I've some celery in the fridge and anyway, I don't really like cream. I'd rather have cheese than cake, to be perfectly honest, but then it's not my birthday, its George's.

Now, let's get the nozzles out. If I can: the utensil drawer has started to stick, and the light's gone in the bottom oven. Funny how things suddenly start falling apart – one moment everything's completely functional, absolutely normal, the next it's all coming to pieces in front of your eyes. The handle came off the cupboard I keep the mugs in the other day, and the InSinkErator has stopped working.

Bingo. OK, icing time. I wouldn't normally do fondant icing on a Victoria sponge, but I want a really smooth surface so I can pipe George's birthday greeting more easily. I've got a special decorating pen for writing messages on cakes, it's got a sort of pump-action handle that makes it easier to control the flow of icing, stops the wobbling. I want this birthday greeting nice and clear.

Right, I'm going to roll out the fondant icing, and once it's about three millimetres thick I'll use this dish as a template, cut around it, and then the circle of icing will fit neatly on top of the cake. Obviously I need something sticky to make the icing grip to the top of the cake. Normally I'd just use some jam, but I've decided to go a bit more exotic this year and use this tinned stuff.

'Who needs an electric tin opener?' said George, but he got me one anyway, a couple of Christmases ago. I think he bought me a diary too; he can be a bit mean, can George.

Take yesterday. I know he doesn't really like Lenny, but I didn't think he disliked him. As I've said, Lenny keeps out of George's way, and yesterday I realised why. I was standing at the kitchen sink; the roasting pan had been soaking in Fairy Liquid and hot water since I'd removed our Sunday-lunch leg of lamb – all studded with garlic and sprigged with rosemary, delicious.

Anyway, there I was overlooking the back garden. George was dead-heading some roses, when I saw him bend down to pick up a fluorescent yellow tennis ball from the flower bed. His face was crimson by the time he managed to haul himself upright. 'Here, Len' – he didn't shout, he spoke as if they were having a conversation, and he threw the ball. Well, Len was thrilled, he bounced down the garden, fetched the ball and brought it back to George, who took the ball from the dog's slobbery gums, wiped his hand down his trousers in disgust and kicked poor Len hard in the ribs.

I dropped to my knees. I knew he mustn't see me, I knew I couldn't say anything. I pretended I had a migraine and went to bed early – but really I just lay there seething. When George nipped to the pub I phoned Liz.

It's a good brand of dog food, this, beef and rabbit in jelly, but a bit chunky so I'm giving the lumps a good mash. I could always put it in the blender, but I think I've got the consistency just right now so let's coat the cake in this lovely meaty mixture, shall we?

Hmmm smells divine, George, bursting with Omega 6, you lucky boy. Right, now that's done let's pop the lemon fondant on the top and then all I've got left to do is pipe the message. Once I've washed my hands: we don't want rabbit gravy in the icing.

I've gone for a dark orange icing in this bag, it'll complement the lemon fondant. The nozzle is as thin as a nib. The trick is to only breathe once you've finished a word, so here goes, in my very best handwriting:

> Happy Birthday George
> 60 today
> Goodbye
> Bea

I shan't be putting any kisses.

It's over. I'm going to stay at Liz's; I packed the car earlier. I'm not even going to wash up, sod it.

Just need to find the – dammit, where is it? Ah, there it is. I've got the lead, now all I need is . . .

'Come on, Lenny, come to Mummy.'

15

Holiday Letdown

The boys were only small when we first hired this place. Someone at work recommended it, said it was idyllic, and it was, right on the beach, a bit basic, but brilliant.

Sam must have been about six, which means Fergus would have been four, the two of them in their tiny blue shorts and brightly coloured T-shirts.

Fergus had this habit, he used to suck the neckline of his T-shirt. I'd forgotten that, how soggy they were, all stretched out of shape. It was hot back then, we had to chase them with sun-tan lotion. Sam was so fair when he was a little boy. Sad, isn't it, how very blond hair always turns that nasty nicotine yellow? Fergus has always been darker; he's got his father's colouring.

They both wore those elasticated canvas pumps. I was

forever tipping sand out of them. It was so easy that holiday, an ice cream and a football, fish-and-chip suppers, the two of them falling asleep at the kitchen table with ketchup mouths. Ben and me carrying them up to bed, two little sacks of potatoes, two bedtime stories before Ben and I could untangle their little grass-snake arms from around our necks and settle ourselves outside in rackety old deckchairs. Warm summer nights with a bottle of wine and a bag of pistachios, watching the sun go down.

Sam lost his first tooth here.

We kept promising to come back but I kept leaving it too late in the season to book, because when Fergus started school I went freelance and could never get my timings right.

The flyer was on the wall for ages: 'Two-bedroom holiday cottage to rent, no mod cons.'

You're not kidding.

A few years later I lost that piece of paper. It disappeared when we had the kitchen redecorated, chucked out with all the other stuff that had been pinned to an old cork notice-board. Endless scraps of paper, all those reminders of dental appointments, kids' birthday parties, all the stuff of young family life.

I used to be so in charge. I used to know everything that went on in my sons' lives: they relied on me to take them to swimming and judo; they needed me to make sure they had their reading books and recorders.

I think I liked it. I liked making sure they had clean socks and healthy snacks, plastic plates of chopped apple, little cubes of cheese and a handful of raisins. In the evenings I'd stand over them while they sat two in a bath, flannelling the backs of their grubby necks, making sure they were clean behind the ears.

My sons, their eyes so clear, Sam's a steely blue-grey, Fergus's Coca-Cola brown, the bath water bobbing with plastic toys, boats and dinosaurs.

Ten years ago since we were last here, then. There have been other holidays since, mostly abroad, because without having to try too hard we started doing quite well.

Ben got a better job, then another one that was even better, and more by luck than judgement we moved into the right area at the right time and found ourselves surrounded by lots of other people just like us. Young families who lived in houses a bit like ours and drove similar cars; some even had children with the same names as our two.

These people became our friends. It was inevitable, we squeezed out the singles and the weirdos and none of us thought we would ever be lonely again.

There were a lot of Sunday lunches followed by wellington-boot walks in the park, scooters and roller blades, we even got a dog. 'Boys should have dogs,' Ben said, but it wasn't him who had to walk the thing.

I was always a bit frightened of it. Sometimes, when we were alone in the house, it would growl at me unless I sat stone-still on the sofa, and once, when I bent down to stack the dishwasher, it sort of bit my nose. The boys thought it was hilarious.

There isn't a dishwasher here. I didn't notice that the last time we came, I just saw the sea and the beach, the vast expanse of safe sandy play space for my growing lads. I saw sandcastles and buckets full of hermit crabs.

The dog died last month. It's a terrible thing to say, but I was relieved. I just didn't need any more on my plate; it was one less thing to worry about.

I left it at the vet's wrapped in a blanket that, halfway home, I realised I really liked and almost went back to fetch.

Mallorca, Minorca, Portugal, blinding bright sunlight places with sand so hot it burnt your feet. We often went with a group of our friends, the 'usual crew', shared fincas, lilo fights, a posse of kids staying up way beyond their bedtimes, little Playmobil people scattered everywhere, umpteen empty bottles on the patio in the morning.

We were boozy then without remorse, without guilt, fizzy Spanish beers at lunchtime, cheap six o'clock cava.

We were a gang; some of us were even successful. We worked in TV and for national newspapers, we were the Boden-wearing middle classes at play. Our children were at good schools and in the process of having their teeth straightened: nothing could go wrong that couldn't be fixed.

I have the photos of last year's holiday on my phone, barbecue evenings reflected in a sinking orange sun, jaunty straw hats and designer sunglasses. Look how everyone is smiling, even Sam and Fergus. Their noses are freckled and their shoulders rosy.

Ben has brought a bottle of whisky with him. I catch a whiff of the remnants in his glass; it smells of peat, like a freshly dug grave. The bin is full of empty tins of lager – which reminds me, I need to take the rubbish out. If only it would stop raining, but it won't. It hasn't stopped raining since we arrived. The boys are still asleep, but the rain woke me up. I could feel the damp. Our bedroom stinks of it, mildew in the corners, my husband unshaven and snoring.

I wonder how many other families have been here since we came ten years ago. Quite a lot, judging by the wear and tear. I have become used to more up-market accommodation with sleek kitchen work surfaces, shower fittings designed by NASA and heated towel rails. Here there are stains that no amount of bleach and scrubbing can undo, purple felt-tip scribble on the landing wall, splashes of orange nail varnish on the bedside table.

The bookshelf in the sitting room is warped and full of discarded holiday reading: an odd mix of chick-lit covers with metallic titles, ancient Agatha Christies and at least two copies of *The Girl with the Dragon Tattoo*. My sons only read their phones.

As a child, I loved weather like this. I used to pull my bedroom-window blind all the way down so that it made a tent with my single bed inside it, and I would read for hours, jam on buttered crackers, a mug of hot Ribena.

There is no PlayStation here, no Xbox or Netflix, but there are board games in a cupboard in the sitting room, Cluedo and Monopoly, Scrabble. I wish we were the kind of family that could play Scrabble together. Imagine if we could just light a fire and talk and play Scrabble and listen to the radio.

I would have to pay my sons to do that. I would have to bribe them with money, shove cash into their sweaty

hands, and still they would yawn at me, their big teenage mouths gaping in boredom, dingy unbrushed teeth and eggy breath.

Sometimes, close up, I find them rather ugly, these sons of mine: Sam's fat nose, pitted like a strawberry with black-heads, the ridiculous fluff on his upper lip, the boils on Fergus's neck.

Fergus is better-looking than his older brother, but there is something rat-like about him. He is furtive – you can't trust him near loose change on a kitchen table. Neither of them will do anything for anyone unless there is something in it for themselves.

The grease is thick on these plates. I had cheese on toast for supper last night. The rest of my family ate a Chinese takeaway: it's the only place for miles that's open after 6 p.m. I can still smell the chemicals, the sauces thick and shiny with the monosodium glutamate I'm allergic to.

Ben doesn't believe me. He thinks I'm being neurotic, which is a bit rich coming from a man who went through a very 'organic' phase just a few months ago. Weeks of skinless chicken breasts, protein shakes and wheatgrass. Taking his cycling deathly seriously, clicking around the kitchen in those ridiculous cycling shoes, leaving bits of squashed fruit all over the place. My husband transformed into a knotted string of lean muscle and lycra, constantly strapping on that stupid pointed helmet.

'Where are you going?'

'Out.'

'Out where?'

'Training.'

I don't remember this place being so poky. My sons seem disproportionately large in these low-ceilinged rooms. They have to remember to duck every time they come into the kitchen.

'Mum, where's the Coke?'

I dislike them drinking fizzy drinks as much as I dislike Ben drinking whisky, but after all we are on holiday, which means crisps and Coke and what? These days, the word fun sounds like a threat?

'Some kind of holiday,' sneers Fergus. Neither of them can understand what we are doing here; the television is the size of a matchbox and there is no Wi-Fi, never mind 4G.

They have friends who will be spending this half term abroad, like we did last year and the year before that.

To be honest, we haven't been here for twenty-four hours yet and I dread them waking up. I forgot to bring any Nutella.

They will fill this space with their resentment and my husband will continue to wear his brave face while resolutely refusing to meet my eye and I wonder whether he has always been a coward.

The sea has disappeared. I know it's out there because in the past I have stood at this sink and seen it with my own eyes, but right now I could be in the middle of Birmingham. I think they call it a mizzle – the cloud has sagged from the sky right down to the ground. I might as well have hung sodden grey sheets on the washing line in the garden. The view has been obliterated.

I could make egg fried bread; they used to love that. I need a big frying pan. I'm a bit surprised they don't seem to have updated any of the equipment in here – the toaster looks lethal. There's a washing machine but no dryer, which is useless in weather like this. I like to keep on top of the washing: teenage boys smell, their armpits and feet reek, they fart and shit and barely bother to wipe their own bottoms, not caring that I have to rinse out the evidence.

The doors of the kitchen cupboards stick. Under the sink I find several bottles of Sarson's vinegar, a drum of artificial sweeteners and a jar of freeze-dried coffee gone the texture of mouse droppings.

I can't find a frying pan, and suddenly I am exhausted and I stagger from the kitchen on legs that feel like sandbags and I lie down on the cheap leatherette sofa in the sitting room and I notice how threadbare the carpet is and I think of our friends who will be waking up in a gleaming white villa perched like a sugar cube on the side of a hill.

I visualise an early-morning garden with a sprinkler in the background, splashes of orange hibiscus, and I imagine how within a few hours the poolside will be teeming with teenage bodies, lolling around like seals, flopping in and out of the water, rolling on their bellies into the shade, and for a moment I am tempted to turn on the gas fire.

I sit up and rub my arms; my marrow feels like it needs defrosting. This place is cold and joyless today, and it seems unfair that we must all be punished because one of us has done something so pathetically stupid.

Ben's bottle of whisky is on the table by my elbow, next to the visitors' book. I've always loved a visitors' book, especially one that says Visitors' Book in self-important gold lettering on tooled maroon leather. I like sniggering at the unintentionally hilarious entries written by people I've always felt slightly superior to.

The book is old, and as soon as I pick it up I know that if I flick back far enough I will recognise my own handwriting, those loopy italics that give away my all-girls grammar school education. The school that cost nothing, unlike my sons' education, which despite bringing us to the verge of bankruptcy has barely taught them the rudiments of joined-up writing.

The entry is dated half term, May 2006. In fat purple felt tip I have written,

A brilliant time here at the cove: sun, sea and two very happy little boys, plus a relaxed and smiling mum and dad. Thank you, thank you, thank you, can't wait to come back!

Throughout the book, there are similar comments, 'Super fun', 'What a great place, chucked it down all week but we had an excellent time!' 'Sad to be leaving, hope to return soon, cheers'. Sometimes a child has contributed, big uneven printed letters jiggling over the ruled lines, 'it was lovely', says Bella, aged six, and she has drawn a sun that looks like a spider. Suddenly I cannot bear that I can't turn the clock back and that even if we survive the next few days there will be a load of crap to face up to when we get home, and before I start crying I snatch a biro from my bag and I write:

Fabulous fun with other half and the 'terrible teens'. Weather mixed, so lots of card games and laughs in front of the fire. Such fun to get away from the internet for a few days – we all feel so much better for it. Many thanks! See you in another ten years, the Johnsons

Of course, I could have written,

Utterly miserable time in this godforsaken dump. No one speaking because my husband fucked up an Ibiza trip by making a pass at our friends' au pair at a recent birthday party. Sorry about the broken glass.

Then I throw the half-full bottle of whisky at the wall and I walk out into the rain.

Carol Goes Swimming

It was the nurse who made me come. You know that face they do when they're taking your blood pressure, one eyebrow disappears into their hairline and they say, 'Would you like to calm down for a moment?' Which is medical-speak for, 'Well, this is borderline stroke territory.'

She's as fat as I am, but I know I'm going to get the lecture: my cholesterol is too high and my blood pressure's through the roof. 'Do something cardio,' they say, 'but be careful.' In other words, don't blame us if you cark it on the cross trainer. Anyway, I hate gyms, the smell of them: the sour, sweaty desperation of puffed-up men and spotty boys with cheesy feet and low self-esteem, who think if they change themselves on the outside, then they'll be different on the inside.

I used to be in better shape – I've let myself go. It's easily done, the kids leave home, the dog dies and the next thing you know, you're looking into a Quality Street tin full of empty wrappers.

Anyway, nursey says, 'Do you enjoy any physical activities?' I say, 'I like sex [which is a lie, I'm not fussed about it], ping pong, and I knit.' She's got a packet of Hobnobs tucked behind the files on her desk. Crumbs all down her front, she's as bad as I am, but because she's wearing a white coat we have to pretend she's not a size eighteen with puffy ankles.

She says, 'Well, knitting isn't going to get your heart rate going much faster!' And I'm thinking, You've never come a cropper attempting a Fair Isle sweater on circular needles, but I wasn't there to chat. I was there for my annual MOT, and so far I was failing. Then she says, 'What about swimming?' And, well, that's why I'm here, because I remembered how much I liked it, back in the day. Mind you, you didn't need a pound for your locker back then.

Chlorine and bleach, the smell never changes. I remember first coming here with my school when I was seven. I couldn't get my tights back on after the lesson. The panic, all damp legs and twisted grey wool, a girl in my class with red hair laughing at me nearly half a century ago.

I've only got fifteen minutes before they shut. I like it when its quiet; I like catching the tail end of the Tuesday-night ladies-only session. All sorts of women, all different shapes and sizes. You forget to care what you look like. I'm in a size-sixteen hibiscus print I bought for the Canaries a couple of years ago. February sun my foot.

Some of the Indian ladies swim in saris and cotton legging

things, and of course the Muslim girls are all covered up, but they all squeal and splash and roll around like puppies in the water. Fat, thin, old, young, you can't be depressed in water. It buoys you up, physically and mentally.

Me and Sandra taught my kids to swim here, and after we'd buy a loaf of seeded bread from the Turkish shop over the road and the kids would tear it apart on the way home, Lindsay and Joe bickering between mouthfuls. Later on we went through an aqua aerobics phase. Our Thursday-night treat, Sandra called it, aqua aerobics then straight round to Bartholomew's wine bar. Bottle of Soave, wet costumes in rolled-up towels under our bar stools – we were always having to go back for them. It's a phone shop now.

At least they've done this place up. Lottery funding. Still gets grubby, mind. At the end of the day, like now, there's a faint grey tidemark around the white tiles. It's the schools, kids not properly washed before they come. Never mind. If I lie on my back I can see the inky sky through the windows in the roof, and I think about how long I've lived around here and how everything changes and yet it's still the same.

Victorian originally, this place – they've got some black-and-white photos in the entrance. It was an old laundry and bath house, and during the war they kept it going in case the fire brigade needed the water. Funny how history gets more interesting the older you are. When you're young you don't care.

They've kept all the fancy wrought iron, patched up all the crumbling plasterwork. Germolene pink it used to be, all cracked and peeling. White now, like a clinic.

In the water, I am weightless. I could be in space. My mind flits: pictures and memories, me and Sandra taking the kids to the park, that time our Lindsay got poison ivy, little Joe doing a nativity, my dad and his allotment, trying to like cauliflower, my wedding shoes, Sandra and me just laughing at nonsense. It all comes and goes like blinking, nothing really joined up, and I know I should be on my front, doing my breaststroke, counting my lengths. Not just lolling here on my back, remembering when I was young and the backs of my legs weren't all quilted with cellulite and people hadn't started dying.

I'm the last swimmer in. Two girls all covered in tattoos got out as I got in, inky shoulders, inky ankles, art school types. Sandra had a butterfly, left shoulder, got it done in Camden Town. I was going to have a matching one but I bottled out. 'Ooh Caz, you big chicken,' she said.

I can't be doing with coming in the morning. That's when the serious swimmers come, the men carving up the pool doing butterfly, I ask you! A woman wouldn't do that. I swim apologetically, 'Sorry if I kicked you, sorry my toe got you in the gusset, sorry.' I'm much more polite in water than I am on dry land.

They flick the lights when they want you out, like a pub in the old days. 'Come on, let's be having you.' My uncle had a boozer over in Bermondsey, died of cirrhosis of the liver. Nose like a massive red sponge, all the warning signs were there, but he took no notice. Like Sandra: she told me in the end that she'd felt something was wrong for months, just never got round to doing anything about it.

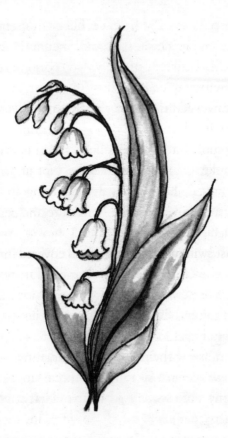

It still makes me angry. That's why I've got to take care of myself, that's why I go for all the check-ups. I've seen what happens if you don't.

I'll finish this length and then I can pull myself out by the shallow-end steps. Heave ho, old girl. I always mean to bring flip-flops – verruca germs all over. Our Lindsay had them. She was always a one for funny things, Lindsay: poison ivy, verrucas, impetigo. She's a solicitor now, but when she gets nervous she pulls out the hairs on her right eyebrow. That's how I can tell if she's been stressed: if her eyebrows have got the mange. My lad Joe is in IT, which comes in useful when we need to retune the Sky box.

I have to be careful not to waddle as I walk back to the changing rooms. I'm on the verge of being that fat, but not yet. I try to walk with purpose, belly in, arms swinging, like Captain Mainwaring in drag, but the tops of my legs chafe and I can't wait to get properly dry. I do need to shower and condition my hair, mind. The boiler's gone dodgy at home and I'm not taking the risk of a cold shower when I get in. Anyway, if I don't condition I look like Worzel Gummidge.

Dammit, the cleaner's in the showers. I'll sneak in after she's gone, give myself a right going over with the L'Oréal, cos I'm worth it. Ha, I wish. Couple more swishes of that mop and she'll be done. They never get right into the corners, and who can blame them? It's a crappy job and no one gives you any credit. If I just sit tight she'll not see me round this corner. I don't want to be told I can't use the facilities. I've not come here to argue.

I used to say that to my kids, whenever we went anywhere and they'd kick off. 'I've not come here to argue.'

Sandra never had kids. Shame, she had more patience than I ever did. We never discussed it. I didn't think she really minded, but when Marco left her, he had twins with his new girlfriend and she just said, 'I always knew deep down there was something wrong with me.' I told her not to be silly.

Like a mermaid she was back then in this pool, long red

hair streaming out behind her, all freckles and green eyes like a cat, bit of Irish from way back. Her sisters looked nothing like her. She was a one-off, the kind of woman other women noticed and men didn't approach. After Marco there wasn't anyone for years. I didn't get it, she was such a stunner, but my old man said she wasn't the type men went for: all teeth, nose and hair. He said he was a bit scared of her. She drank whisky and smoked roll-ups and looked like she was laughing at a secret he'd never understand, but the kids adored her. Auntie Sandra made up the best stories, carved a pumpkin better than anyone and always knew where to find the frogspawn.

I never knew anyone with more life in her than Sandra. If it wasn't for her, I'd have been a dull girl. She made me do things I wouldn't have done by myself, like the rotor ride at Battersea fun fair, the one where the world drops away from your feet and you're left stuck to the wall of a big drum by whatsitsface – centrifugal force.

She made me go to Glastonbury with Joe still in nappies, and that gay bar in Vauxhall where we took little blue pills and I was sick all the way home. I never thought there'd be a time when I wouldn't see her. Long legs, big feet, I always remember my dad looking at her feet and saying, 'She'd not sink in a desert.' Big as a camel's, but not as hairy. We were in the same class at primary; she was the girl that laughed at me getting into a knot with my tights after swimming. Inseparable, that's what they called us.

I still look out for gingers. You see them in parks, standing out like red squirrels amongst all the grey ones. There's a lurch in my heart when I see curly red-haired girls with cross faces and ginger biscuit-crumb freckles. The ones that won't get off the swings, or insist on riding their bikes through mud. The difficult ones that won't give in.

Oh come on, woman, hurry up, I'll catch my death sat here in a soggy swimsuit. Only I won't, will I? No one dies of a soggy swimsuit, not in this day and age.

I never thought she'd give in. That was the shock of it: I thought she was too stubborn to die. I still can't believe she's gone. I see her everywhere, I call out to strange women in the street and they turn around, and they're ten years younger or they're wearing glasses and the wrong colour lipstick and I feel quite cross. Even though it's not their fault that my best friend died and left me. It's still unbelievable because the clues of her are everywhere: the rollerblades she bought our Lindsay still in the garage, the hat she bought for me in Bruges. Every time I make a fish pie I can hear her singing 'She shall have a fishy in a little dishy, she shall have a fishy when the boat comes in' in a really bad Geordie accent because it made me laugh.

Even now, in this changing room, there's a hair bobble on the bench next to me, tangled strands of knotted hair the same shade as hers, auburn with copper highlights, and I tell you I could weep. I could cry every time I see something that I want to tell her about. I still can't delete her number on my phone and sometimes I still smell her, a great waft of lily of the valley, cos even when she was totally skint she'd never put anything but Diorissimo behind those great big ears of hers.

Oh come on, Carol, this won't buy the baby a new bonnet. No good getting morbid. The cleaner's finally gone, put up the wet floor sign. I need to get home, it's cod loins in breadcrumbs and oven chips tonight. In any case, they'll be wanting to lock up. As my Uncle Bob used to say, 'Chop, chop, let's be having you.'

Only I got up too quick, didn't I, and it was like being on the rotor ride again. I'm dizzy but there's no centrifugal force to keep me upright. I feel the blackness before I feel the floor and I know that I'm fainting because it's happened before, only not when I've only got a swimming cossie on and then . . . Nothing.

Apparently I must have hit my head as I fell. Out cold, they said, only not for long. The manager was leaning over me when I opened my eyes. She had a name tag on, 'Brenda Bailey Supervisor', and she said, 'Hello? Hello, can you hear me? You've taken a fall, love. I think you might have hit your head on the bin here. Can you hear me?'

I could hear her, but I couldn't be bothered to tell her. I was lying on the floor in a wet swimsuit and my teeth were chattering I was that cold.

She was kneeling on the floor next to me, rubbing my shoulder trying to warm me up. 'I've got you covered, love. Towel and a blanket, see? I don't think you've broken anything, but you might have a bit of an egg on your head in the morning. Anyway, the paramedics are on their way, we'll get you sorted.'

I told her I was sorry, but she wasn't having any of it. She said, 'Oh don't be daft, it was an accident. Mind you,

I was just about to set the alarm and lock up. The cleaner had finished in here. I thought everyone had gone. You could have been here all night – good job your mate was with you.'

Well, that didn't make sense, because I'd come on my own.

'What mate?'

And this Brenda Bailey just goes, 'Tall woman, striking. Red hair.'

And for a second I could smell her, the sweet scent of lily of the valley, and then she was gone.

17

Waiting for Billy

Billy's gig is not going well. I can hear what's going on through the backstage tannoy, and it's embarrassing.

Oh come on, you lot, wake up. Give the man a break – it's like a bleedin' séance out there. We sat in stinking traffic for two and a half hours to get here, wherever this is.

I turn the tannoy right down. I can't bear it. As soon as I hear him sing 'Sweet Patsy' I know it's interval time. I reckon another fifteen minutes or so. I don't watch him any more – I've seen the show a million times and anyway, I've got series two of *Peaky Blinders* on my iPad. No Wi-Fi mind – typical.

Patsy Gordon, this is your life, sat on a plastic chair backstage with a packet of cheese and onion, listening to the old man try to whip a load of corpses into a frenzy.

Just under a hundred in tonight, but mark my words, he'll

still come off that stage sweating like it was Wembley. I can't even have a drink, cos I said I'd drive back – poxy door split doesn't warrant stopping over in a decent hotel and I'm sick of Premier Inns. I want a massage and room service, not a blinking KitKat out of a machine down the hallway.

Me and Billy used to have the lot. Serious like, massive house in the country, lake with them koi carp all gliding through the murk. Used to make me feel sick, like someone had put something in the water and turned goldfish into these humungous monsters. Mind you, I took a lot of mind-altering drugs back then – I should be ashamed to say, we both did. Billy bought a hot-air balloon once, and we kept peacocks. Someone said they were unlucky, but I think most people have their ups and downs. Though when I think about it, me and Billy, we've been hit by lightning flying over the Indian Ocean; robbed at gunpoint in the Miami Hilton – every ring off my finger. I tell you, if they'd known I'd had a diamond in my belly button they'd have had it – not that I did. And we've had every health scare under the sun. Bill's been clinically dead twice, but at least once it was his own fault.

My old mum used to say, You're a magnet for trouble, Patsy Gordon. I probably got it off my dad. Mind you, I only saw him a couple of times. Brixton nick – it was the only time my mum ever knew where he was.

I don't miss the old place. Have you heard the racket peacocks make? Listen, I can do an impression: *ca-caaaaaaaa* – that's one of my party pieces. I used to be able to pick a credit card up off the floor with my teeth and all, but not any more. I try and keep myself trim. I do pilates – beg pardon, I fake pilates. Mostly I just lie on a mat at the back of the class pretending to engage my core, but secretly just thinking about stuff and how it all happens.

There was this little cottage on the edge of the estate, and I wish we'd been able to keep that.

I tell you, where we live now is smaller than the place we kept the lawnmowers. Two of them – Billy used to race them. That's what did for the carp in the end. They were big fish, but you can't argue with an electric lawnmower. Sunday lunchtime, terrible mess. Course I'm going back a few years, when there was money. Show business isn't what it used to be.

'Move with the times,' that's what Billy's agent says, so he did a reality show a couple of years ago. I think he'd have done quite well but he got bitten by some weird kind of spider and his arm went black and they had to get him out of there. Come to think about it, Billy's not good with wildlife. Someone poisoned the peacocks – great lump of poisoned meat, didn't even bother to mince it up for them, just chucked it over the wall and bingo, Elvis and Cilla dead in the back yard.

Course we had staff to deal with that sort of stuff, burying peacocks and the like – a gardener and housekeeper. Sometimes it's like looking back on someone else's life, only I know it's me because I'm there in the photos: floppy hat, sitting on the wall overlooking the rose garden, shadow of my legs by the sun dial, having a fag on the croquet lawn. I did some modelling, but mostly I was with Billy and the boys.

I miss the band cos it was a bit like family, though some of the other wives drove me nuts. Mostly because they kept changing. Suddenly all the Paulines and Sues became Ingrids and Birgittas, then there was a time when the tour bus was full of little Japanese birds. Tiny shoes, like dolls. Just me and Billy left of the originals, like a rock and roll Darby and Joan.

I've always travelled with him. I used to pretend I was like a mascot, but really it was so I could keep an eye on him. I used to see the other boys come down for breakfast, groupie guilt written all over them. Once had to find the drummer a clap clinic in Düsseldorf. All the other wives stayed home with the kids; me and Billy were going to adopt, but we never finished the paperwork. I'm glad really: I'd have been stuck at home, Billy would have done something silly, I'd have found out and divorced him out of spite. Mind you, I'd have been better off if I'd divorced him when he was loaded. Billy's old bass player Mick, his first wife Tracey still lives out in Marbella, but his third wife, Hoshiko, lives with Mick and his mum in a flat down the Cally Road. Ex-local authority. Mick bought it off the council for his mum back in the eighties. Never thought he'd end up living there.

I've been with Billy since I was nineteen. I help him with his image, choose his stage clothes: black jeans, long black coat. He wanted to wear a hat – he's always liked dressing up. I told him he'd look like a fat highwayman. He likes hats cos his hair's thinning. He's been to the same transplant fella as Wayne Rooney, but it's come through very fine. Cost a fortune. To be honest, I'd rather he was bald and we could afford to go on holiday, but as he says, it's just him up there and there's no light show to distract them – mostly we just have a mirror ball and a bit of dry ice.

He's a solo artiste now. Not much choice: everyone else is either mad, dead or not speaking to him. Ninety-minute acoustic set, bit of banter about the old days and Bob's your uncle, back in the car and home to the dogs. I thought maybe I'd breed Afghans, but Billy's allergic so we've just got the two Jack Russells.

Billy says a gig's a gig, but I remember when they were massive in Europe and Asia, and they'd have a chef backstage, cook anything the boys liked – which was mostly chips and beans. We could be anywhere, from Moscow to Melbourne, and this fella could cook anything. En croute this, flambé that, but they just wanted what their mums would have cooked for them when they got in from school. Islington boys: you can take the lads out the Angel, but they'll always be on the lookout for some pie and mash.

Beers and lagers before the show – keep it light, otherwise there'd be fights on stage – wines and spirits after. Course Billy still gets a rider, I see to that. It's in his contract: selection of sandwiches (no tuna, it repeats on him), fruit bowl, tea and coffee, bottled water. Some places they do it nicely, others don't even hoover out the dressing room – you can always tell. A dried-up contact lens curled up on the carpet, mic tape stuck to the mirror, wig and eyelash glue. Depends who's been on the night before. We play the regions, a few arts centres, seaside resorts, all the dives. What's that old joke? 'As they say in showbiz, you play so and so twice in your career, once on the way up, once on the way down. Good to be back!' Same acts going round in circles. Lots of comics – young men, skinny jeans, big hair – telly psychics, bit of what they call spoken word.

Billy's kid brother used to write the lyrics; Larry had a way with words, always kept a diary. I had a soft spot for Larry, but I wouldn't have gone near him if Billy hadn't pigged out on the Jim Beam and passed out. Thirty-odd years ago and I still blush. Sometimes I'm glad Larry's dead, cos now it can never come out. I used to live in fear, all them Sunday dinners: pass the salt, and by the way I slept with your missus. I tell you, the relief when the band split up and Larry married a Kiwi girl and moved out to New Zealand.

Mind you, Larry weren't like that, he was a very sweet man. The only one that never tried to sue Billy over non-existent money. It was the last album that did for them. I never really understood it – in between record companies, decided to go it alone, recording studio in Barbados and of course it went and burnt down. Spliff-related, no doubt. Every single thing up in smoke, then they had to cancel a tour because Mick and the drummer were in a car crash, collarbones in smithereens, and my mum said, 'Patsy, you're like something out of *East Enders*.' Well, I can't be doing with it no more. I'm all for a quiet life, just me, Billy and the dogs.

We didn't have kids because of medical reasons. I knew it must have been Billy's fault because after I slept with Larry I was pregnant. I knew I'd never keep it. I went to stay with an old school friend on the Isle of Man. Only I never did, I went to a clinic in Birmingham. I wore a blonde wig, looked like one of the Birgittas, just distanced myself from the whole thing. Don't know why I'm even thinking about it now. It's just Larry died a month ago and I didn't even go to the funeral because we couldn't scrape together the airfare, not unless we both went economy and really, I don't know how people do that. So just Billy went. I think he was looking forward to it – not the funeral, I think he just fancied the flight. Twenty-four hours in business class with a stopover in KL like the old days. Malaysian Airlines, all hot, scented towels, chicken satay skewers and free booze, what's not to like? Course, Billy don't drink no more. Once upon a time they'd have poured him off.

Been ages since I got off a plane and saw a different sky, felt a different heat. I even miss Billy being a drunk sometimes. Be nice to share a bottle of wine, Sunday evenings in front of the fire, good bottle of Merlot. Trouble is, Billy could never stick to the half bottle. Once he started he wouldn't stop, drank 'til he swallowed the worm at the bottom of a bottle of Mezcal. When in Mexico, and all that. Course he was warned. At one stage his liver looked like a bit of steak that had been char-grilled on a barbecue. There's none of the other stuff neither, no drugs apart from statins. Billy's weakness now is battenberg and ice cream; he's borderline diabetic and his cholesterol's out of control. Be typical after all the other stuff, all the drink and the class As, if it was the pudding that got him in the end.

Still a shock that Larry died first. He was in better nick, taller, slimmer, more hair on his head. His wife is in bits. Billy phoned me when he got there, said it was a beautiful place right on the beach, great big wooden veranda looking out at the ocean, and I think about our crummy little gaff on a bend in the main road and the bin lorries and the beep-bleedin'-beep of the Morrisons delivery truck and I wonder, what did I do to deserve this?

He just didn't wake up one morning, aneurism, but at least he never suffered. Course, Bill's drummer Nobby died in bed and all, but only cos he fell asleep with a fag in his hand and next thing you know it's duvet inferno, poor bastard. Mind you, Nobby by name, knob by nature. He really was a terrible prick.

Larry was a gent. His missus wanted to give Billy all his old notebooks: boxes of 'em, diaries, scraps of unfinished songs, doodles and stuff. Would have cost a fortune in excess baggage, Billy said, so he decided to burn 'em: bonfire on the beach the day after the funeral. He said there were too many words, said looking at the pages made him feel tired, said it made him angry. I think Billy feels bad about being the

172

one left behind. He's been proper moody since he got back. Honest to God, it's me I feel sorry for, living with a miserable teetotal, non-smoking, fat boring git, bless him. Oh come on, Bill, must be coming up for the interval by now. Let's have a check.

He wrote 'Sweet Patsy' for me when I was twenty-six; number one in seven different countries, punters love it, makes 'em feel young again.

I whack the tannoy back up. He'll do a bit of patter, song and off. It's a bit crackly but I can just about hear him, and he says, 'I thought I'd play you a new song tonight. Only just wrote it, so it's fresh off the back of an envelope, seriously. Some of you will know my brother died and, well, I went out there and I wrote this. It's called "And I Found Out".'

I turn the tannoy right off, because I don't want to hear it, but it don't make much difference. I've got a racket in my head like you wouldn't believe and I don't think I'll ever hear 'Sweet Patsy' again. From now on, I think I'm just going to be stuck with this other noise. It's like the peacocks are back, and that's all I can hear, peacocks screaming like a warning.

18

Leo's Passport

Quarter to six and my hands are sweating like onions in a pan. At six o'clock I shall put on my coat and I will walk out of here, and no one will ever guess that it was me. I wish I didn't feel quite so sick – oh dear, this is all so difficult.

I have worked in this office for many years. Brewster and Crowley is a very established firm of family solicitors. I'm part of the furniture, only they've recently changed all the furniture, knocked through to what used to be a fruit and veg shop next door, had a complete makeover. It looks like a clinic now, one of those places that offer fillers and Botox in your lunch hour. People must look in and wonder why they've got some old trout sat answering the phones, like a permanent 'before' fixture.

It used to be all dark wood panelling and magnolia

woodchip. Easy on the eye, some nice prints of seasonal woodland walks. Not any more: it's halogen lights and silver patterned wallpaper. I'd say I get three migraines a month as a result. Some days I'm tempted to sit here in reception wearing my sunglasses, but I don't because I'm a professional and Leo's so thrilled with it.

Leo Brewster. I used to work for his father, straight from school nearly forty years ago. Office junior, did a secretarial at night school, learned how to be indispensable. I may not be decorative, but I'm efficient and reliable. 'Don't you dare even think about retiring, Penny,' says Leo. I have a horrible feeling he thinks I'm older than I am. Most people do: every time I go down to my local baths they insist on giving me the over-sixties silver swimmer rate. I'm only fifty-six.

He says losing me would be like having his right arm cut off. He doesn't mean it: he'd manage perfectly well, he's a very competent man, very successful – hence the expansion and the fancy lighting, the silly squiggly paintings and the expresso machine. 'Espresso not expresso,' says know-it-all Jodie. It's got one of those hot-milk frothers, bit spitty. Personally I can't see what's wrong with a kettle and a spoon-ful of Mellow Birds, but apparently we are moving with the times.

Which is why we had our Christmas do in a Mexican tapas bar. 'Spice up your life, Penny!' screamed Jodie, blasting garlic right into my face, and I must have looked a bit blank because she then started explaining that not only was 'Spice Up Your Life' the title of an early Spice Girls hit, but her own personal life philosophy.

I said, 'I'm well aware of the Spice Girls' oeuvre, Jodie, but I can't see what's festive about patatas bravas and cod balls.' Suffice to say, I was not *having a good time*. I'm not a fan of the serve-yourself buffet, I'd rather a sit-down hot turkey dinner with all the trimmings, but oh no, the entire office, plus the Croydon branch, milling about with sangria moustaches, no crackers and a DJ! I ask you. You don't need a DJ at your Christmas dinner, you want a medley of festive hits, preferably with a few carols chucked in.

I can feel myself perspiring and I hope to God there are no visible damp patches. I wish I had my lucky lump of Blu-Tack, but since the renovations I'm not allowed personal effects on my desk. Apparently photographs of dead cats, the *Star Trek* mug that I kept all my pens in, and my grubby lump of Blu-Tack, which I was fond of squeezing when stressed, look out of place in this new streamlined office.

The only thing I am allowed is the plant Leo's wife bought me for my birthday. An orchid – white, as luck would have it, came in a nice ceramic pot from Marks with a card: 'To Penny, with all best wishes for a happy birthday. Regards, The Brewster family'.

Very nice woman is Caroline Brewster, very well-mannered. Always asks after my father and I say, 'Thank you, Caroline, he's as well as can be expected given the circumstances.' Because no one wants to hear the truth, do they? No one wants you to turn round and say, 'Oh how's my dad? Well, you know, up to his usual tricks, the piss-sodden devil: wetting the bed, shouting at the telly, wandering around the neighbourhood in his filthy pyjamas

and chucking his dinner at the wall. Mad as a badger but as strong as an ox. In fact, he'll probably see me out. Cheers, and thanks for asking.'

She's got enough worries of her own, has Caroline. That's why I did it; I don't see why she should have to put up with any silly nonsense on top of what she's already got on her plate.

Of course Leo's allowed photos on his desk, because he's

the boss and anyway, he's got them in proper silver frames and not rubbish plastic things from Argos. There's a lovely one of Caroline taken about three years ago, she's looking really happy on a beach in Sardinia building an elaborate sandcastle with their little girl. Amy, she'll be about twelve now. She's another reason why I did it.

I know all children are supposed to be precious, blah blah, but Caroline went through five rounds of IVF to get Amy. She told me in confidence a couple of Christmas parties ago. We might have had a drink, and she asked me whether I'd ever wanted children. I said my dad and the cats were enough of a handful, and she laughed and said that Amy was a miracle of modern medicine and that she'd never wanted something so badly in her life. Then she got a little bit emotional and I had to lend her my hankie, which was a tad embarrassing as I'd had a very heavy cold that week and it wasn't exactly clean.

I tried not to look shocked when I saw her next, only I barely recognised her. She certainly didn't look like the same woman who was laughing on the beach in the photo.

I can't remember what it's like to feel warm sand between my toes. To be honest, I can't remember what it's like to have any kind of holiday, not even a weekend – or a *mini break*, as other people call them. Oh we're going to Oslo for the weekend, oh I'm kayaking in the Dordogne this bank holiday, oh we're nipping over to Dubai, winter sun, yak, yak yak. I get so tired of hearing about other people's lives.

Jodie is one of those girls that always has a tan. Fake, of course, like her so-called designer handbag and her silly shoes and her ridiculous laugh and her stupid mobile phone with all the shiny crystals on it, like she thinks she's a pop star when all she really does is chase up legal documents and make phone calls about outstanding fees.

Leo called her a breath of fresh air when she first started working here. That upset me because it made me feel like somehow I was the opposite, a shapeless lump of a woman in a semolina-coloured cardigan constantly leaking some kind of stale, inert gas. Which I don't, because I am vigilant about hygiene. I know how badly my father smells and I won't let that happen to me. Mints in my handbag, fresh-breath spray and, if possible, I leave the office to let off. Unless Jodie happens to be walking past, in which case I let one fly in her direction, because there are only so many ways one can voice one's disapproval, and as we all know, actions speak louder than words.

Sometimes it's a combination of both, isn't it, actions and words, and when the penny finally dropped I couldn't have been more disappointed in Leo if he'd been my own husband. And I haven't got one of those, as people are so fond of reminding me. 'Oh but you're not married are you, Penny, you don't have a husband, do you?'

'No,' I feel like screaming, 'I don't have a husband, but I have got a cat who disembowels baby birds and leaves the chewed-up remains on my sofa, so I know what it feels like to be let down by someone you love.'

We're all just animals really, aren't we, ruled by our instincts. We're all capable of behaving badly. Sometimes I am cruel to my father, I push him that bit too hard, squeeze his wrists, and then I can't bear to look at him for a couple of days, see the confusion in his eyes. Mind you, he's always confused. I don't think he's any idea that it's his own daughter that's being mean to him. In his eyes I'm just a horrible stranger, which is a relief in some respects.

She was losing her hair the last time she visited, Caroline, just popped in to see how the renovations looked. You could see she was tired. Jodie made her a cup of coffee, which I thought was a terrible cheek, treacherous really, smiling that bleached smile of hers, fatty lips all shining with the goo stuff she's forever slicking round her mouth. 'No, you sit down, Mrs Brewster, really it's no trouble. Are you sure you don't want a biscuit?'

I should have said, 'You want to watch this one, Caroline. If she has her way, the next time you see her will be in the divorce courts, because she's digging her claws into your husband and I don't know whether they've slept together yet, but last week she bought a pair of lace-topped hold-up stockings from Marks ... And there's you, Caroline, looking all washed out, but I suppose that's chemo for you ... '

We handle a lot of divorces in this office, lots of red-rimmed eyes and terrible language. Sometimes Leo doesn't shut the door to his inner sanctum and you can hear it out here: 'The shit ... that cow ... my life is ruined'.

Of course it's very good business for us, because once the divorce has gone though there's all the consequences to deal with: the selling of the matrimonial home, the dividing of the assets, the custody of the children to sort out. Oh yes, Brewster and Crowley do very well off other people's misery.

Which is why I was so surprised when I found out about Amsterdam. Jodie and Leo are going tonight – they're on the 9 p.m. flight from Gatwick. There are two small flight cases out in the corridor. Travelling light: no doubt her case is full of silly underwear, push-up bras and ridiculous G-strings. At least Leo's bothered to buy a guidebook, and yesterday I heard him singing 'I saw a mouse. Where? There on the stair! Where on the stair? Just there, a little mouse with clogs on,' which would have been funny if he wasn't about to make the biggest mistake of his life.

So that's why I did it. Leo has kept his passport in the office ever since we started doing the renovations. He needed it to get large sums of money out of the bank on a Friday to pay the builders and never bothered to take it home. It's just sat there in the top left-hand drawer of his desk for months.

So last night, while he put his coat on and sang about a mouse going clip-clippety-clop on the stairs, I held back, pretended I had a few emails to send, said that I'd see to the locks and the alarm. I'm often the last one out because I don't have anyone to rush home to, and, unlike Jodie, I don't have constant appointments to get my legs and lady bits waxed and my eyebrows coloured in like two big slugs across my forehead.

So I waited until I knew that everyone had gone and then I simply removed the passport from the drawer and took it home. I hid it in the airing cupboard, I don't know why. He was born on the 28th of July 1963, his middle name is Paul and, rather disappointingly, Leo turns out to be short for Leonard.

And I laughed as I tucked the passport between a stack of pillowcases, imagining Jodie shouting 'Leonard, oh Leonard!' whilst in the throes of passion. Which, thanks to me, will no longer happen. Ms Jodie Robbins will have to entertain herself this weekend. With any luck she'll drink her body weight in Jägerbombs and fall into a canal – she strikes me as being silly enough not to have learnt to swim.

My dad taught me. I have to remember sometimes that he wasn't always useless; there was a time when he could fix anything.

The taxi to the airport is booked for six. I heard Leo – or should I say Leonard Paul, which makes him sound more like a hairdresser than a solicitor – tell Jodie this morning. She kind of squealed, all high-pitched, like a pig trapped in a barbed-wire fence, and said, 'I'm so excited, I can't wait. Are you excited?' And he said, 'Yes, I've been looking forward to this for weeks.' Honestly, I almost brought my breakfast up.

I might leave five minutes early; I've been feeling nauseous all day. Jodie's in the bathroom, no doubt bronzing her cheekbones with that dark metallic glittery stuff that bears no resemblance to any living flesh tone, not unless you have the complexion of an aubergine, and spraying herself with that disgusting scent of hers that stinks like a sweetshop after a fire.

I'm just gathering my bits to go when someone outside presses the intercom. It's five fifty-five, so whoever this is will get short shrift, but considering I'm still officially on duty I answer the wretched thing.

'Hello, Brewster and Crowley.'

I recognise her voice as soon as she speaks. 'Penny, it's Caroline.'

'Oh, Caroline,' I say, 'just push the door.'

Well, what else can I say?

She looks a lot better; her hair is growing back, soft pale brown feathers in a sort of pixie crop, eyes shining. She looks excited. Leo appears in the corridor; he's wearing his coat, and he says, 'Darling, you don't mind if we give Jodie a lift to the airport, do you? Only she's on the same flight as us – some hen do. Silly not to share. I just need to grab my passport.'

And, as quietly as a mouse, I get my coat and I leave.

19

Doing the Best for Daniel

He was three weeks early, but that's Daniel for you. I was relieved because it meant he was a Pisces like me. I've always felt very spiritually connected with Daniel; it's always been just me and him. Obviously he has a biological father, but some things just aren't meant to be and in the end Daniel's daddy decided to stay with his wife and daughters.

I can't say I wasn't devastated at the time, despite all those declarations of undying love and future plans whispered across his polished mahogany desk as we frantically undid each other's buttons between meetings with his clients.

I was a junior clerk in his chambers. I arranged his diary and every day I arranged a minimum twenty-minute love-making window. But in the end it wasn't enough. He stayed with Sonia, who prefers that Daniel's contact with his only son is kept to a CSA minimum.

Yes, I called him Daniel after his father. I figured if his father was going to deprive him of his rightful surname, he couldn't stop me using his Christian name. I like to imagine that Daniel senior is reminded of his son every time someone calls his name. It must be a constant reminder, like gravel in his shoe. I hope it hurts.

These days Daniel junior likes to call himself Danny or Dan, but I don't. His name is Daniel, Daniel George. It's a good name, respectable, it doesn't shriek 'illegitimate, daft cow of a mother – got caught out by the boss, oldest trick in the book'.

I don't mind telling you it was tough: baby, no job, one-bedroom basement flat out in Eltham, mould up the inside of the curtains. But eighteen years on, Daniel and I are very comfortable. I am the living proof that not all single mothers scrounge off the state. Some of us earn fifty-two thousand pounds a year and have a selection of Mulberry handbags to prove it.

Don't get me wrong, I don't have money to throw around, and anyway, Daniel comes first, always has. I realised he was bright before he could walk; he had a look in his eye – inquisitive, like a squirrel. All the other kids looked dull by comparison. Oh, some of them were up and running before Daniel: I met a woman whose son was walking at nine months, but as I said to her, 'He's probably going to be sporty. My Daniel's a thinker.'

Though as it happens, he's gifted at sport too. He's been

on the swimming squad since he was fourteen and his tennis shows a great deal of promise. I'm just glad he doesn't play rugby. The last thing he needs before he goes to university is a head injury.

That's why today is so important. I couldn't sleep last night, I felt physically ill and I don't drink as a rule, but I took a handful of Kalms and went to bed with a large Baileys. It's times like this that I miss having someone to talk to. Of course I know some of the other parents at school, but it's not like we're a big gang of mums hanging round the gates. It's not like it was at primary and even then I was forever working, clawing my way up the corporate ladder for Daniel's future, so he had an au pair. Not that she was foreign, and she didn't live in either. I called her an au pair because it sounded more professional than a childminder. Amy Glossop, she had a 2.1 in history from York University and specialised in the Tudors. She didn't stay long; none of them did. It didn't bother me, I didn't want my child forming emotional attachments with surrogate parents, but I didn't mind him learning. After Amy I employed a lot of recent graduates, particularly those with useful degrees such as Latin and further maths. We had a quantum physics MA student once: clueless about stacking the dishwasher, but he taught Daniel how to construct an atom out of a balloon and some frozen peas.

By the time my son sat the entrance exam for the local high-flying fee-paying boys' school he had, courtesy of the au pairs, decent conversational French, a smattering of Mandarin, fluent cricket lingo and a passion for the films of Jacques Tati. He won a full scholarship, no thanks to his father, who had paid for both daughters to board at Cheltenham Ladies'. Ladies, my foot. One's a deadbeat cokehead and the other is clinically obese. Not that I've met them, but Facebook has made private detectives of us all.

I wonder if his father cyber-stalks Daniel, spying on a life that he's had nothing to do with. Look, there he is skiing. I paid for that trip, you didn't. I have been doing the best for Daniel ever since he was born, just me and nobody else.

As soon as he could sit up, I didn't waste a moment. Alphabet flashcards when he was on the potty, times tables tapes on the way to nursery, Gustav Holst's *The Planets* on the way back. I bought him a flute, and as he got older I sacrificed beach holidays for traipsing around Pompeii. I have overdosed on borscht and dumplings in Russia in aid of his GCSE history paper, and suffered daily palpitations whilst he climbed Kilimanjaro because I thought it would look good on his UCAS form.

I've fought for my son to have the finest education surrounded by boys from good families, parents who belong to golf clubs.

I don't come from this. You don't get life on a plate when you come from Croydon. I might not get invited to these houses with gravel drives, but my son does. I've made damn sure I've given Daniel what his father owes him.

Obviously I can't compete with the oligarchs and City fathers, the hedge fund dads and Bentley-driving record company managers. I know the stakes are high. There are birthday parties in marquees, invitations to second homes in Cornwall; last summer my son caught marlin off Cape Cod. But he is as good as any of them. Better than most, with their rounded shoulders and greasy chins. My son is clever and handsome, his hair is as arrogantly thick and blond as his father's, he is blessed with clear skin which tans easily in the sun, he looks like a young Kennedy, he could do anything.

Which is why I don't understand his behaviour. Today my son gets his A-level results. The most important day of his newly adult life, and he decides to have a lie-in. He is predicted all As; I am hoping for all A-stars. I couldn't eat breakfast; he mashed up three Weetabix and sat in his underpants playing stupid music through his headphones. Didn't even look at the time.

From eight o'clock, they said. I'd taken the day off work – I wanted to drive him, but he said he wanted to go on his bike. I don't like him having a bike. He doesn't wear his helmet; he pretends to, but he doesn't. Sometimes I don't know him.

I want my boy back. I want my little boy with his dinosaurs and dressing gown, not this six-foot stranger.

Anyway, I followed him. I've parked my Nissan round the corner from the school. He has to come back this way, and I should be able to tell from his face. I need to know. I'm hunched down low behind the wheel so he doesn't see me. I thought about wearing a pull-down beanie hat, but it's August and I'm soaked with nerves.

Everyone else is just going about their business: a middle-aged couple walking a fat spaniel; two girls lounging around on the lawn opposite, a dirty blonde in a vest and shorts, her mate in a skimpy floral dress over a bulging bikini. They shouldn't be on that grass. It's private property, it belongs to the school. It might be the summer holidays, but they've no right to be there. The blonde one has kicked off her flip-flops as if she were in her own back garden. Honestly, it's not on.

I've got a good mind to beep, but they look the type to give me a mouthful. St Hilda's girls, no doubt – they tend to be on the slaggy side. Oh don't get me wrong, I'm sure they do their best, but they have a lot of problem families.

Ugh, the one with the bare feet is rolling a cigarette. Dirty dyed yellow hair in her eyes, scraggy-looking thing, wouldn't be surprised if there was weed in that roll-up. I bet I could smell it if I rolled down the window, but I can't. Sitting here with the glare of the sun bouncing off the windows makes it harder to see me. Oh come on, Daniel.

I'd like to take him out tonight – me, my son and a bottle of champagne – but he's already told me Adam's having a barbecue. Adam Ellingham-Tate, big barn conversion, heated outdoor pool. Adam has a place to study medicine at Bristol; his father is an ear, nose and throat man – as I say, it's the crème de la crème at that school. One of Daniel's mates is the great-great-great-grandson of Lord Cardigan, who led the Charge of the Light Brigade. These are my son's friends. No glue-sniffers or thieving toe-rags – the college is no St Hilda's, I'm very relieved to say!

She's knotted her top under her grubby bra, the thin one. There's something tattooed to the side of her belly button, eyeliner smudged under her eyes. The big one does a clumsy handstand, fat thighs wobbling. I can hear them laugh, it goes right through me. The blonde reaches into a plastic bag, gets out a Diet Coke and a tatty copy of *Heat* magazine, and they lie on their fronts on manicured grass that they have no business to be anywhere near, looking at pictures of brain-dead celebrities. Silly girls, tiresome.

If Daniel gets his As he will study law at King's like his father. He can still live at home, I can still take care of him, make sure he has a decent breakfast. He doesn't want to be worrying about the supermarket when he has a lot of studying to do.

Sometimes I have this fantasy that Daniel is a defence barrister and he is standing up in court against his biological father, who is representing the prosecution, and Daniel, in his new wig and gown, trounces his father, leaves him blustering, tongue-tied and confused – like I was the day he said he wasn't leaving Sonia. Sometimes I imagine Daniel senior has a heart attack with the shock of it and Sonia cries and cries. After all, she is still very young to be a widow, and what is she going to do? She's never worked a day in her life. I hate Sonia.

Oh come on, Daniel, this is torture.

Oh dear, oh my Lord.

He coming, he's wheeling his bike. That's Nathan Burrows he's with. Nathan is grinning like a hyena – he would, he's got an unconditional offer from Warwick, PPE. My son is looking around. For a moment I think he is looking for me. Of course he is: I have been by his side through everything, the day he got his letter from the college, the words 'we are pleased to offer' dancing across the crested paper.

It's always been just me and him, me traipsing up the stairs leaving glasses of ice-cold milk and cereal bars outside his bedroom door while he revised, gently knocking on his door – not disturbing, just supporting. Me making sure he has everything he needs, the laptop and iPhone, his trainers, the lights for his bike, his new bike. He is propping his bike up against the fence, he is slapping Nathan on the back, he is jogging over the road, leaving his brand-new bike unlocked.

Oh God, in a moment I will know. It's like giving birth, the split-second between not knowing and finding out: 'A son, you have a son, a beautiful baby son.'

My chest feels tight even though I've removed my seatbelt. I am stationary but I feel like I'm hurtling towards something. He is jogging . . . to the girl. He is picking up the blonde girl, he is swinging her round, the dirty girl with the grass-stained shorts is clinging to my son like a tarty octopus, her arms around his neck, her bare legs locked around his waist. They fall, of course they do – stupid cow could have broken his neck – and they crumple in a heap on the grass. The fat girl laughs in a stupid hysterical way, jumps up and down clapping. Suddenly she checks her watch, looks over her shoulder at an approaching bus and trots, flat-footed, to the bus stop. The scruffy one sits on top of my son, she holds his hands above his head and leans down as if to kiss him. The blood is pounding in my head and I cannot breathe, I wind down the window and the words come out of my mouth.

'Get off him! Get off my son. How dare you—'

My son rolls over and stands, his head swivelling until he recognises the car. He looks straight at me. He doesn't speak, but his face tells me everything I need to know. I can see it in his eyes. My son has got his three As; he can take his place at King's but he won't, he will take up his other offer, at Edinburgh University. I can read the decision as if it were written in capitals across his face. My son wants to get as far away from me as possible, and it is all my fault. He bends to help the girl up, whispers in her ear. She looks around, confused. He leads her to where he left his bike, steadying her as they step over the chain-link fence that she should never have crossed in the first place. He puts one hand around the naked flesh of the girl's waist and steers his bike with the other, and together they walk away in the opposite direction.

20

The Viewing

'Call me Damien' is a boy in a suit – a lot of them are. Poor thing, twenty-five and already his hair is thinning. It's people like me who make it fall out. He knows I'm wasting his time.

I hope we haven't met before. I try to be careful: I use different offices, I don't stay too close to home, I'm very polite. I make sure they can't really say no. None of them have so far.

Lots of people have strange hobbies, don't they? Grown adults who dress up in animal outfits, men who pretend to be babies, women who make greetings cards from craft kits they buy off the internet. As long as no one gets hurt, then I can't really see the harm.

Damien says I have fifteen minutes before the 'next lot'

are booked in. He's agitated; his BlackBerry keeps cutting out – the signal is obviously very weak in this area. I think that's a useful thing to know, but there's no mention of it in the particulars.

Poor Damien, he keeps having to go out into the front garden to finish his calls. Doesn't bother me, I'm perfectly content to see myself around.

Victorian end of terrace, four bedder, £875,000, architecturally enhanced. Like a woman who's had a load of work done, the glass kitchen extension being the Victorian semi's answer to having a new set of boobs. Everyone's doing it. Of course there are pro and cons: lots of extra light, but not great when an incontinent pigeon flies overhead.

Sliding doors out to the garden. It's what young women want, isn't it? Pink-cheeked children playing in the garden while Mummy makes something nutritious and yummy for tea. They expect a lot, these well-married mummies with their pasta machines and jugs of filtered water. This one's got one of those espresso machines. Two kids, I'd say, all the usual clues: Wendy house in the back garden, the obligatory red and yellow plastic slide, fridge covered with nursery-school drawings, a group portrait of a stick family is entitled 'Jamie and Freya, Mummy and Daddy'. A grown-up has obviously done the writing; the crayon people are all massive heads and balloon hands.

Whilst Damien is in the front garden yapping into his mobile phone and pushing his poor hair off his forehead, I open the baby-blue fifties-style fridge-freezer, the kind of contraption that looks like a small Cadillac parked in the corner of the kitchen. You can tell a lot about people from the contents of their fridge, and their medicine cabinet and their knicker drawer for that matter.

The fridge surprises me. Women who live in these kinds of houses tend to like a full fridge; their reputations as loving wives and mothers depend on abundant bags of spinach, oily fish and goat's cheese. Goat's cheese, despite tasting like condensed bile, is very popular amongst the chai latte classes of this newly gentrified area of south-east London. Oh and hummus, the middle-class standby. Hummus and pitta bread, the twenty-first century's answer to bread and dripping.

This fridge is bare save for a quartet of Munch Bunch yoghurts, a packet of salami, a heel of parmesan and three eggs. Rather than the usual organic meat there is a stack of ready-made children's meals. Someone's obviously given up, I conclude, feeling like Miss Marple. After all, you are what you buy in the supermarket. For example, my shopping basket often contains just three items, gin, biscuits and cat food, but then I am a single adult with no dependents relying on me not to develop scurvy.

Of course, if I were a mother I would take my shopping more seriously, plan menus and keep novelty-shaped biscuit cutters for baking days. I would shop in delicatessens instead of picking up most of what I need from the Texaco garage down the road.

Damien has lit a cigarette. Good, it gives me more snooping time.

The sitting rooms are cool and tasteful, the walls painted in what might have once been called magnolia, until magnolia became naff and was reinvented as cloud or parsnip, or cream of cauliflower. In my experience, the more expensive the paint, the dafter the name.

Anyway, it's a symphony of string and biscuit shades made less bland by some big splashy paintings and a vast deep turquoise velvet sofa, one of those come on kids, let's all cuddle up numbers. Suddenly I can see them, a jumble of family in pyjamas. I can imagine where they would put the Christmas tree – a real one, naturally, they are that kind of family, Mummy and Daddy, Jamie and Freya.

Mummy and Daddy are perched on the mantelpiece, looking ecstatic in a silver frame. An arty black-and-white wedding photo, a blur of confetti, the newlyweds laughing into each other's eyes. I tell you, it's enough to make you puke.

A cluster of smaller frames reveal the children to have grown from purple scrunched-up goblins into cheerful-looking dark-haired toddlers. The girl is more watchful than her brother. He is younger, a face-pulling boy trailing a felt monkey.

Damien catches my eye through the front window. If I lived here I'd want more privacy, but then happy people have very little to hide. They probably like the idea of people looking in and seeing them all loved up, drinking hot chocolate on the sea-blue sofa.

By rights they should have a dog. I haven't seen any evidence, but I think something small and bouncy would suit them, a terrier maybe. I feel a wave of irritation. How come these people don't have a pet, not so much as a goldfish? Then I reason that one of the children might be allergic. Immediately I picture the girl with an inhaler, little Freya, wheezing in the night, calling out for her mummy.

They've gone for a rather jaunty stair runner. Multi-coloured stripes, not wool; it's that stuff that feels more like string. Very hard-wearing, apparently. Well, you'd need that with the children. There's a grey tidemark up the wall, grubby toddler hands unable to reach the banister rail – for some reason the sight of it makes my heart lurch.

I imagine they're quite sociable, these people. They will have friends, other young families, who live locally. I bet they all meet up for muddy walks on Sunday mornings before coming back here. The children will take their wellingtons off in the hallway and charge around the house, and there will be a big roast lunch, lamb I think, all studded with garlic and rosemary like in the magazines. I'm sure she cooks some-times. She must, that kitchen isn't just a stage set.

Four bedrooms. The children's are small and at the back of the house, one is yellow, the other orange – obviously they're trying not to gender stereotype, which is admirable, but the duvets are a giveaway. The boy has a Thomas the Tank Engine cover, the girl's is pink with white stars all over. A line of dolls is tucked under the duvet. She has closed the lids of the dolls with working eyes; only a balding insomniac teddy lies wide awake, one glass eye drooping on his furry cheek.

It's much easier being a child, isn't it? You're positively encouraged to live in an imaginary world, to make-believe and pretend. It's only when you are a grown-up that pretend-ing is viewed with suspicion and those of us who would rather live in our heads than the real world are thought peculiar.

The boy's room smells faintly of urine, as if someone has had a recent accident. A large plastic container on wheels overflows with the stuff of small boys' dreams: dislocated Action Men, a thousand Lego pieces, the tracks of a Brio train set. More touching are the soft toys, a menagerie of velvet pigs and fluffy lions piled high in a wicker basket. A small pair of barely worn black shoes with Velcro straps stand stiffly to attention in the corner.

The bathroom is next door. With any luck that boy will soon learn to make his way to the lavatory in the middle of the night instead of pissing where he sleeps. But then I remember what it was to be scared of the dark, of the bogies and the monsters under the bed. Again they've kept the bathroom decor quite neutral. The mosaic tiles are the same biscuit shades as downstairs, vibrant towels are new but badly folded over a heated rail.

I haven't heard the front door, so I'm presuming Damien is still outside. I open a cabinet attached to the wall, a square white metal box with a red emergency cross on it. Nice touch, I haven't seen one of these before. Inside are all the usual supplies for your bog-standard family illnesses and injuries: plasters, TCP, Bonjela, paracetamol, Deep Heat, a rolled-up crepe bandage, some Rennies, a tube of Berocca. So far so normal. Only the packet of prescribed sleeping pills seems out of place. The prescription is dated very recently and made out to a Simon Ritter. Oh dear, poor Daddy is having trouble sleeping, whereas judging by the stash of sodium citrate sachets, Mrs Ritter is obviously prone to cystitis.

I take a swig of Rescue Remedy, which I find tastes exactly like cheap brandy, and close the metal box.

In the master bedroom, I sit down on the bed. Snooping can be quite tiring. Sometimes, like now, I feel defeated by this compulsion to see how other people live and I question why I do this, why I rub other people's normality into my own face.

Why do I keep needing to compare what other people manage to achieve, houses with new towels and children and tastefully chosen paintings and cushions, to what I have, which is some cats and a small rented, furnished flat complete with a peculiar peach-coloured bathroom suite?

These beds are known as sleigh beds, they originated in the nineteenth century. This one's a reproduction, but it's good, and the polished mahogany glows. I would sleep well in this bed; I can't understand why Simon should have any problem. He keeps a pair of John Lewis tartan pajamas under his pillow, there is nothing under hers – she must sleep in the nude.

A stale glass of water on his bedside table, on her side there is a Venetian glass box containing a rather gruesome child's milk tooth and a white leather frame containing one of those taken-at-sunset photos. Mrs Ritter and her husband are leaving footsteps in the sand, the sky is scarlet and gold behind them, she is wearing a swimming costume – just a plain black one, the kind of costume you can actually swim in – and a butterfly-print sarong around her narrow hips. I'd say she was a tall size ten. He is even taller, six foot and smiling in a pair of red shorts. You can see the boy in him: this is what Jamie will look like when he grows up. The girl is a mix of the two of them, her father's curls, her mother's eyes.

In the romantic evening stroll photo, the necklace Mrs Ritter is wearing is strung with delicate shells. It's the sort of necklace that is designed to look homemade, but is actually rather pricey. I feel the irritation rise again, the familiar bitter taste at the back of my throat. This woman has everything, she has a four-bedroom house with off-street parking in a desirable area, a state-of-the-art kitchen she can barely be bothered to use, two petless children, one of whom is a bed-wetter, and a husband who cannot sleep without resorting to medication.

From this evidence I can deduce that Madame Ritter is either a bitch or a cow, or perhaps both. I know I shouldn't, but I slide my shoes off and I curl up under the Ritters' duvet. I would like to stay here for ever.

The sound of the front door pulls me up. Voices in the hallway, a woman's and a man's – a couple no doubt hoping to progress up the property ladder. I can guess without looking that she will be pregnant with baby number two. They want more space, a bigger garden, blah, blah. Life really can be such a cliché. Quickly I put on my shoes, poke my head over the banister rail and tell Damien I'm nearly done. It's a shame I won't have time to root through her wardrobe: I would have liked to have helped myself to a small memento, a scarf, perhaps. I find it quite easy to steal from people that I feel do not deserve their good fortune.

The fourth bedroom is actually a study. An entire wall of old orange Penguin Classics. A twenty-seven-inch screen Apple Mac looks well used, but the calendar pinned to a cork board behind the computer is stuck on December.

It's March now: after all, spring is the season to start selling houses. Below the Matisse print, in the grid of December dates, amongst the scribbled reminders for drinks with Sam and Rosie, and Jamie's school nativity, the word HOLIDAY is spelt out in thick black marker pen, followed by three exclamation marks.

They obviously went somewhere on the fifteenth. Skiing maybe, isn't that what moneyed young families do? A creak on the stairs alerts me to Damien and the prospective buyers making their way up to the first floor. I hover on the landing. It's bad luck to cross on the stairs, and because I don't need any more crap in my life I tend to be overly cautious.

A fair-haired woman leads the procession. I'm right, she is pregnant. Damien is behind her and, bringing up the rear, is a beaded red-haired man looking for all the world like a Norwegian trawlerman.

The pregnant woman is obviously impressed. 'I just can't understand why they should want to move, not when they've just got it so lovely,' she says and Damien replies, 'Yeah well, it's all a bit tragic, to be honest. They were on holiday and, er . . . Australia, and there was an accident. In the sea, what they call a rip tide, and Mrs Ritter didn't make it. They're moving nearer to his parents.'

'Oh God,' says the blonde woman, 'those poor little mites.' She walks past me, presuming I must be the cleaner or something, whilst Damien gives me a look as if to say, 'What are you doing here, you freak?' Which is a look I am quite accustomed to.

I wait until the stairs are traffic free and then I disappear back to my own life.

21

Sitting

I travel free, of course. One of the perks of being ancient is that I can roam the metropolis at will without being charged a single penny, although now and again I find my right arm instinctively raises itself in what could be interpreted as a sympathetic gesture to the Nazis, when in reality I am just hailing a cab. Extravagance is permissible when it rains, when my feet hurt and if I just want to sit alone in private.

Although these days I have plenty of time for sitting alone in private. I've lived by myself ever since my husband died. It's been five years and I still haven't got round to doing anything with his ashes. The urn is wrapped up in an Edinburgh Woollen Mill plastic bag, which is quite apt I suppose, what with him being an Angus. We honeymooned in the

Highlands, over half a century ago. I got bitten very badly. I thought, really, if I'd wanted to come home from my holiday covered in angry red lumps, then I might as well have gone somewhere exotic for them. He liked fishing. I sat silently by the side of lochs, being bitten. I was a good wife, and when our son was born some forty weeks after our wedding night, I was a good mother.

Bus to Sloane Square, Tube to Victoria, train to Denmark Hill, all for nothing, and then I walk. I have always liked to walk. After Angus died I got a little rescue dog for my daily constitutional. A dachshund, I called him Bobby. He was a very good chum, if slightly low to the ground. It was a good job that Angus was safely turned to powder in his urn; he would have spent the entire time tripping over him. He was a big man, ungainly, clumsy. Our son inherited the same ridiculous feet. After Angus died I wanted something small and dainty around the place. Neat little smooth-haired Bobby was ideal, but he didn't live long – some kind of doggy cancer – but I knew exactly where to scatter *his* ashes: he's in my window boxes. A lot of people admire my geraniums and I always say, 'Well, it's thanks to Bobby', and they think Bobby must be a gardener. Though why anyone would need a gardener in a third-floor flat is beyond me. I never used to take the lift but these days I do, especially when I've been to Waitrose. Anyway, it's useful for visitors: some of my friends are really quite decrepit.

People let themselves go at an alarming rate these days. Travelling across London on public transport, I see the most extraordinary sights. Young women literally spilling out of their clothes and yet still eating, holding brown paper bags of greasy snacks, feeding their fat children sugar-coated doughnuts. Sad, really. I have always been careful with my food. Portion control, that's the trick, small plates, tiny spoons, and I drink in moderation, although when one lives alone it's difficult sometimes to know when to stop. I have taken to rationing my gin by drinking it out of eggcups. Sometimes I have six eggcups a night. The girls drink sherry when they come to my place. I still keep a decanter, but I've noticed some people don't bother. When we go to Patsy Openshaw's she just sloshes it out of the bottle. Last summer, when it was very hot, she offered us cold cans of lager, which was very peculiar, but also delicious.

Of course some of the book club ladies stick to tea or coffee or a fruit squash. I always arrange a plate of fancy biscuits on a tray, make an effort, though I draw the line at baking. I threw all that stuff out when I moved: muffin trays, whisks, loose-bottomed tins, I don't need it.

My friends are mostly divorced or widows, and for the most part not too fussed.

I have a photograph of myself on my wedding day, gazing at Angus as if to say, 'Really? Is this really the man I am going to spend the rest of my life with?'

I look aghast, and he looks slightly disappointed.

On the day I married Angus I realised my husband-to-be was besotted with my maid of honour. Walking up the aisle in my virginal white duchesse satin frock, complete with lace veil, it struck me with alarming clarity that he was looking straight past me and into the eyes of my cousin Leonora.

She was very beautiful, but she died of a brain haemorrhage when she was thirty-six, so maybe Angus didn't pull the short straw. What use would the beautiful Leonora have been in his dotage? How well would she have coped with the endless pills and the bed pan?

Never mind 'til death do us part – that's the easy bit. It's the incontinence and dementia that are the true test of a marriage.

As he grew older my husband looked more Scottish, like one of those ginger Highland cows. A very hairy man, all over like a pelt.

We called our son Martin and I never really knew why. I think Angus chose it. Maybe I was meant to get my choice, should I ever present him with a girl, and for years girls names rolled around in my head – Rosemarie Jane, Sophie Elizabeth, Jennifer Emerald – but I never fell pregnant again, and all the nights I lay awake dreaming up names for the daughters I never had I didn't once ask Angus if he was doing the same.

But maybe he was. Maybe he lay there thinking Gregory Paul, Timothy Michael. Who knows?

I do have a granddaughter, however. Her name is Esme, a consequence of my daughter-in-law being Welsh, which, as my friend Aileen Beatty says, could be worse.

Esme is a solid thing with beige hair, which I yearn to cut. One mustn't, though. One mustn't interfere with grandchildren. Once, when my friend Ailsa had her granddaughter to stay while her son's partner got over the complications of yet another pregnancy, she took her granddaughter's earrings out. By the time her mother got her back the holes had entirely closed up. Apparently the woman was hysterical; phoned her up and called her a bitch.

Earrings might cheer Esme up a bit. She really is rather colourless. They've moved out to the suburbs, my son and his small family. He calls it the countryside, I call it the suburbs. He finds London distasteful, all the dirt and the mess. I have a feeling he has UKIP tendencies. He likes village greens and the thwack of willow on leather, warm beer in a silver tankard. I like to be where the action is. I like to watch strangers go about their business. I see everything because no one ever notices me. Old age is a great disguise. People who yearn for invisibility need only wait until their seventies to achieve it.

I don't mind the march of time, but some of my friends rage against it. Patsy wears ridiculous orange lipstick that frays around her mouth, clashing with her yellow fangs.

Dorothy insists on sporting only shades of purple, anything from mauve to plum. Greta dyes her hair an increasingly unlikely auburn.

The rest of us are your average motley bunch of whiskery chins and beige cardigans. Increasingly, there are a number of elasticated knee supports, and poor Hilary Graham has had to start buying her shoes from the chemist.

I still have good legs, but I'm a martyr to heartburn. I've always had a nervous stomach – comes from living with opinionated men. Angus liked the sound of his own voice, and Martin's just as bad. Sometimes when we have book club we talk more about our ailments than the book. Next time it's my turn to choose, I swear I'm going to go for a medical dictionary. We'd get so much conversation out of it. It would be all 'I had that once', 'Well I've had it twice.'

Of course the funerals have started. They all came to Angus's. Dorothy toned down the purples to a respectable, and somewhat apt, deadly nightshade, and Hilary crammed her feet into a pair of patent lace-ups. Her ankles puffed up during the service like dough rising in a low oven. Even Greta had the decency to cover her hair with a very strange-looking lace mantilla. She looked like a geriatric Spanish dancer.

Occupational hazard, funerals, at our age. As Hilary said, 'I'm never out of that wretched black skirt.' Mind you, for a lot of old folk it's a day out, plus you get a sandwich and a nice slice of cake. Saves bothering to have to cook yourself dinner.

I eat what I like now. Angus liked his meat and gravy, but

if I fancy it I'll just have half an avocado. It's not that I have to scrimp – he didn't leave me badly off, and anyway, I earn a bit of pin money myself.

Funny really, I'm seventy-eight and it's the first job I've ever had. Angus wanted me at home, you see, looking after his son and keeping his house tidy.

It's only part time, once or twice a week, and there's a lot of sitting around, but at least I get paid. A lot of my friends are volunteers: hospital trolleys, that sort of thing, meals on wheels, and Greta helps out with a blind lady. None of them earns a penny. Of course I don't do it for the money, that would be silly, although I do use it for treats. Hendrick's gin, mostly; it's a superior brand.

Sometimes, I pour the gin into my eggcup and dip a finger of cucumber into it, which I then suck like a gin and cucumber straw.

Living alone and not giving a monkey's is rather wonderful, which is why I cannot think of anything worse than going to live with Martin and his Welsh wife and that silent granddaughter of mine, who is ferried daily to and from a private school frequented only by nice girls in knee-length tartan kilts.

Apparently the school in the village isn't really good enough. Then why live there?

'Space,' says Martin, and it's true: he has a big garden, a conservatory and a double garage, plus his wife has a sewing and craft room where she likes to crochet peculiar woollen owls. What *is* her name?

Apparently, I could have a granny flat. There is room to

build an extension and I could choose my own soft furnishings. Well, whoop-di-whoop.

You're not getting any younger, says Martin, and I think, No, and neither are you. How strange to be old enough to have a child who is balding. Martin also has a paunch, and last summer needed his varicose veins stripping. While he lay with his legs bandaged from ankle to knee I was in Barcelona with Dorothy, who was a vision in lilac on La Rambla.

'What if you have a fall?' he asks. I say, 'I'd bang on the floor.' I've got neighbours now, proper neighbours above, below and on both sides. When I lived in a big house I didn't know who lived either side of me – mostly American banking families on two-year contracts. People who were too busy to give you the time of day. We should have downsized years ago, but for Angus it was a matter of pride. Silly really, considering he spent the last two years of his life bedbound in the dining room, completely la-la whilst I fed him through a tube.

He shrank then, the Highland cow turned into a little white mouse of a man.

Some of my gang play bridge on a Friday. It's not my cup of tea. I don't want to be organised any more, I don't want rules. Don't get me wrong, I don't mind routine – I like my every other Thursday book club – but I don't want to be told where to sit or what to do, or how to think.

'You'd see a lot more of your granddaughter,' says Martin, which is a lovely idea in theory but in practice involves long silences. Esme is polite but bored, and that makes two of us. And it would give you a chance to spend time with ... 'He mentions his Welsh wife by name, and Lord knows what is wrong with me, but I have forgotten what the hell it is and I have to force myself into imagining writing her a birthday card. Dear ... Morwenna. Happy birthday, with love. Morwenna, of course. I told you: Welsh.

I was in charge of all the birthdays and Christmases. Angus thought it was woman's work, and it may be, but I rarely bother any more. After Bobby died I treated myself to an iPad, and now I send cards online. No more faffing about with stamps and worrying if it will get there on time.

'Yes, Mother, but it's not really the same.' My son's voice, sounding more like his father daily. Disapproving, just one notch below hectoring.

And I agree: of course it's not the same, that's the point. Nothing's the same any more and that doesn't have to be a bad thing. 'Esme likes her birthday cards lined up on the windowsill,' says Martin, which just goes to show how insecure she is.

I sent her a voucher via the internet too. Martin said, 'Yes, Mother, it's all very well, but there isn't an Accessorize in the village, so there's not much point.'

'Let her come to London then,' I told him. 'Put her on a train, I can meet her. It will be our little adventure.'

But Morwenna doesn't think it's a good idea. She doesn't think Esme will be safe.

Silly really, London is full of fourteen-year-old girls, all shapes and sizes, yacking on their mobile phones. Swarms of them, going in and out of school from High Barnet to Blackheath.

I don't feel unsafe anywhere really, not even round here, and this is not exactly a salubrious area. Once upon a time people who lived on my side of the river would never have ventured out here, but it's changing. Another coffee shop seems to open daily, there's a new artisan pizza place and a shop selling bespoke bicycles, which I've just realised is a pun – spokes as in bicycle wheels. I've only just got it and I walk past the place every Friday. Oh Miriam, keep up girl.

Every Friday, down the hill and right onto the main road. The fresh whiff of a nail bar, a gaggle of school kiddies being walked to the swimming pool, young men with beards like Victorian hypnotists, girls with pink hair and tattooed legs – all the things Martin left London to get away from.

It's a fifteen-minute walk from the train station and I miss Bobby every time I see a little black and tan dachshund, but I never really think of Angus.

Every Friday at 1.55 p.m. I walk up these wide stone steps, through the glass doors and into this other world.

The corridors are familiar now, the noise and smell of young people, sweaty trainers, BO, sex and hope, versus the slightly sour scent of dreams already fading.

Up a set of stairs, holding onto the banister. Slightly out of puff, I round the corner and enter the usual room. The light floods through the windows in the ceiling and I nod to the same man that I nod to every week, a man who must be Martin's age, but unlike my son is resolutely tieless.

Silently I edge behind a wooden partition and I take off my coat and my shoes and my skirt and my stockings and my blouse and my bra and I leave them all in a puddle on the floor, and I loosely tie a faded blue cotton robe around myself and I step out.

Today they want me sitting on a chair. It's an easy pose. After all, I'm an old woman, they're not expecting any gymnastics. They just want to see me for what I am, the skin and bones of me.

And as thirty pairs of eyes stare at my old and wrinkled frame I feel stronger than I ever did, more powerful than on my wedding day when my husband looked straight through me, and for a moment I remember my beautiful cousin but I push her away and I think about my son who wants me to sell my London flat and give him the money so that he can bury me alive in a suburban granny flat where I can supply free babysitting should he and whatsherface decide to have a night out, and I imagine my son's expression when I tell him why I don't want to move, when I explain about my friends and my book club and my bus pass and the fact that every Friday afternoon I like to take my clothes off for gin money, and as I picture his face I start to laugh.

22

The Understudy

This room is cosy. By cosy, I mean it's nine feet by seven, but at least there is a bed . . . of sorts. A camp bed, like a stretcher on stumpy legs, rather low down. Once I get on it I find it hard to get off. Sometimes I gently fall to the floor, roll onto my knees and haul myself up from the carpet. I can't say there's a view. I don't think I've ever had a room with a view, not even on holiday. It's the sort of thing you pay extra for, a view of the sea, of lights twinkling. I have lights, as is the tradition. I also have a melamine shelf for my bits and bobs and a chair, a very ordinary chair, the type you might find in a church hall or thrown on a skip. These things don't really bother me. It's warm and dry, and yes, there are a lot of stairs, but the way I see it, every night is like a free workout. I can't pretend I don't get out of puff – I'm not in great shape – but then I don't really have to be, it's not my job. I see all the young ones, eating their fat-free yoghurts, smoking on the fire escapes, picking out the insides of sandwiches and discarding the bread for the pigeons, and I realise nothing changes.

Girls have always wanted to be thin, and she certainly was. Tiny little slip of a thing, could have passed for fourteen when she was well into her twenties. I find that kind of woman annoying, even now. You see them on train stations and at bus stops, baby women, the kind of women that men want to protect: 'Take my jumper, you must be freezing. Put your hand in my pocket.' I once shared digs with a girl who had a whole drawer full of ex-boyfriends' knitwear. She used to get them out and go through them: 'This was Pete's, this was Ian's, this used to be Harry's.' They were like scalps, scalps from M&S, mostly; some were rather synthetic.

I have never been the kind of woman men have wanted to look after.

Take Glen: when I first met him he was rather hopeless. Irish, good-looking, from Dublin, all curls and parcelled up in his mother's hand-knitted navy Guernsey, stinking of roll-ups and Pot Noodles.

I knit – well, I'm trying. I've got a scarf on the go. Apparently Judi Dench does needlework, she hand-stitches little homilies on linen. Swear words, mostly. I like that. There are many reasons why Dench is a national treasure; it's not just because she can act a bit.

We can all act a bit. I had a lot of promise as a girl. Of course, it all started with the elocution lessons: my mother was a snob and she didn't want my father's Black Country

218

accent rubbing off on me. The elocution lessons were a sort of precaution against me sounding common. My mother was obsessed with not being common, which actually meant she was very common indeed. My mother wouldn't find Judi Dench's needlework funny; she had no sense of humour. I think my father was glad to die – it got him out of a lot of little jobs around the house. She was just furious that he was only halfway through cleaning the car. Dropped down dead with a shammy in his hand. What would the neighbours think?

That's why I'm having a little drink. I shouldn't, not on duty, but it's been thirty years since my dad died, and if a girl can't raise a glass of good single malt to her poor old dead dad, then … I've got a sandwich too. I bring one from home: I used to buy one from Pret, but you get more cheese with your pickle if you make your own … and more pickle: my mum's in an old people's home, she doesn't recognise me. Maybe if I was on the telly more she'd know who I was, ha-ha.

I had a lot of promise, that's what she used to say. She'd never go so far as to say I was talented or gifted, but she thought that with a lot of hard work maybe I could teach. I didn't want to teach. Mind you, it's a good job I learned to type: I've done a fair bit of that in my time. Of course, no one needs that sort of service any more, everyone can type. It's the mobile phones, they've made secretaries of us all.

I was going to save half this sandwich 'til after the interval, but I can't tell you how delicious this cheddar, Branston and whisky combo is. I just wish I had some crisps. It would be like a little party.

I went behind her back, did it in secret. I figured, if I didn't get in then no one would ever know, but she opened the letter. She knew before I did. Afterwards, she said she wished she'd put it on the fire.

I liked Manchester. I worked very hard, I read all the books you're meant to read, did my vocal exercises and slept with Glen Rahilly. Lovely Irish fresher Glen. Being in the second year, I had the confidence to persuade him that getting off with me was a good idea. I'd got lucky with my lodgings, my first attic room to do what and with whom I liked, whereas he had a landlady who wouldn't allow women or drink across the threshold. I was freedom. We were together all the way through his first and second year and then I left. You can't stay, even if you would like to, and once you've officially left you cannot sit around in the refectory to keep an eye on your boyfriend. At least that's what I was told.

I really couldn't see the harm, I couldn't see why I wasn't allowed to sit in my favourite corner, drink coffee, chain-smoke and just keep watch – for pretty little new girls.

Beware the wide-eyed first-year fawn women, beware the little posh types that come in from the Home Counties with their summer tans and expensive hair.

I first saw them together in the autumn-term production of *Romeo and Juliet*. He had a tiny ladder in his tights; I concentrated on that while they kissed. Come to think of it, it was Glen who introduced me to whisky. Thanks for the Glenfiddich, Glen.

So I ignored my instincts, accepted my first crummy job and went on tour with a Theatre in Education company. I played an alien with a blue face; the make-up caused havoc with my skin.

In the December, when the schools broke up, I returned to the Manchester flat I shared with my boyfriend Glen.

I let myself in, and they were curled up on the sofa, his suitcase open on the floor – he was leaving for Ireland and Christmas with his folks the next day. She had bare legs;

they'd obviously just got out of bed. She was wearing the navy blue Guernsey that his mother made him. I have mistrusted women in men's clothing ever since.

She cried a lot, and I mean a lot, so that was two of us with swollen, blotchy purple faces. Hers probably went down the next day. I had to pay a dermatologist to sort mine out.

In the morning he went to Ireland and I went to my parents', and by the time I came back to the flat he'd moved out.

That was the last Christmas that I saw my father alive – cheers, Dad.

I finished the Theatre in Education tour and swore never to get in the back of a transit van again. I changed my name for Equity reasons from Elaine Page – because there already was one – to Ellie Pagett, and got an acting/stage manager job in Birmingham.

I think I might have done it to spite my mother. I certainly made sure that when I went home for my father's funeral some of his old Black Country accent slipped out. Her face was even more like a purse than ever. Incidentally, I have found the accent rather useful: I've used it twice in *Emmerdale* and once in *Holby*.

I went back now and then to Manchester. I had friends who hadn't moved on. That happens quite a lot, people get stuck, don't they? I went to the pub that we always went to, the one by the railway line, a tiny pub all wood and glass and kind yellow light. They were still holding hands. We had a nice chat – acting can be a very useful skill. I acted being a grown-up and exchanged convincing pleasantries with my enemy without scratching at her face.

'I still feel awful,' she said. Her eyes brimmed with tears. See what I mean about acting – it's a really good trick, being able to cry at the drop of a hat.

I've always had to use menthol. They manufacture something called a tear stick now, it's cheating, but don't we all?

He looked a bit fatter, like he was drinking too much beer, and his hair didn't seem as thick. He said he was sorry about my dad, which was kind.

'Are you working?' I asked. She answered for him, 'He's got an agent, and he's doing a lot of auditions.' Neither of them asked about me, but I gave the impression I was fine. I bought a round of drinks to show that I could afford such generosity, lagers all round and a little whisky chaser for me, just to take the edge off.

I was relieved to get back to Birmingham. I was doing a lot of workshops, mostly with women's groups, and I occasionally met and slept with men, mostly bearded types – some of whom weren't as nice as they pretended to be. I know for a fact that one of my lovers only stayed over because his bike had a puncture and he couldn't be bothered to walk it back to Edgbaston at 1 a.m.

Basically, I got on with my life. You do, don't you?

I heard they were sharing a flat in London. Her father had bought it as an investment, in Islington, apparently. Once when I was browsing the *Stage* for jobs, I came across a review of a fringe production in which apparently she 'radiated the innocence and beauty of a freshly bloomed rose'. I nearly gagged.

'Pretty is as pretty does,' my mother used to say – which was as close as she could ever get to apologising to me for not having handed on spectacular looks. I realise now that I was an attractive young woman, and I have the photos to prove it, but somehow I rapidly slid from young female lead into the character section of the actors' directory *Spotlight*.

A friend of mine saw him at a Granada TV casting. They got down to the last three for *Coronation Street*, but the other bloke got it, I tried hard to feel disappointed for him. She was at the National, a very small part, 'but acutely observed', according to *The Times*.

I'm sure he went to meet her every night, I'm sure they held hands as they walked back across the river, I'm sure she told him it would all be OK and that he really shouldn't worry, only maybe he should go to the gym?

The next time I saw him was on the telly. I had to look twice. It was a commercial for a mouthwash; apparently he got paid a fortune, but you'd want a lot of money to be labelled the man with the very bad breath.

He shouldn't have done it; leading men don't have halitosis. Then his mother got ill and he went back to Ireland, and he took over the farm and married the girl he kissed when he was seven and had loads of children and lived happily ever after. Only he didn't, he blew his head off in a cow shed.

No, he didn't, he did the wife and kids thing and, as far as I can tell – and it's difficult to snoop when someone isn't on Facebook – he's well enough. Sometimes I imagine his children, all in navy Guernsey sweaters, though they will be grown adults by now. The eldest will be the age his father was when I first met him, and the idea of that makes me feel cold.

She did well, of course, that combination of cheekbones, a modicum of talent and a shovelful of luck. West End, sitcom, ITV's best-loved female vet, adoring mother, BAFTA winner, *Strictly* runner-up and *Good Housekeeping* cover girl, comedy, tragedy, stage, screen and occasional Radio 4 drama. I saw her on Lorraine Kelly the other morning, saying how thrilled she was to be doing some Shakespeare again. Honestly, you'd think she was doing *Hamlet*. She's playing Juliet's nurse; we all get round to playing the nurse in the end – this is my third time. Not that I'm playing the nurse, I'm understudying the nurse and Lady Capulet and Lady Montague.

She doesn't remember me. We pass on the stairs – her dressing room is conveniently situated at stage level, mine is right here at the top. I'm tucked away, under the eaves, like a servant to be called upon should I suddenly be needed.

I won't be, they're all in, and earlier than normal because it's press night. She was signing autographs at the stage door when I arrived. 'You are sweet,' she was murmuring to a man who looked and smelt like he'd not changed his clothes since his mother laid them out for him back in 1975. As for Mrs Capulet and Mrs Montague, both had already signed in and I could smell Mrs Montague's fish pie emanating from the green-room microwave. She's a bit antisocial like that, is Sylvia.

And they're off, or near as damn it. It's a very bog-standard production; I'm expecting a raft of three-stars. I shan't stay for the party. To be honest, I'm feeling a bit queasy and I seem to have forgotten my contact lenses. I've normally put them in by now, just in case. Let's face it, they didn't have a Specsavers back in sixteenth-century Verona.

I can slip out at the interval, get home and finish my *Borgen* box set.

I'm having one last swig of whisky when the tannoy splutters back into action: 'Miss Pagett to the stage, please. Miss Paget to play Juliet's nurse tonight. Miss Pagett to the stage.'

Apparently shock can be instantly sobering – but sadly not in my case. If I could have escaped through the window without killing myself I would have done, but instead I sat on my chair and tried not to fall off.

A knock on the door. 'Miss Pagett?'

There is a well-known theatrical adage that insists the show must go on, so I did. I went on, I made my West End debut, not that I can remember much about it. But it made all the papers, which made for interesting reading.

I think this cutting from the *Daily Mail* possibly sums the evening up most accurately:

The much loved actress Debbie Hall was taken to hospital last night, suffering from a suspected kidney infection. The production of *Romeo and Juliet* which Ms Hall was scheduled to appear in went ahead, but descended into chaos when the understudy, who appeared inebriated, mistimed an entrance, tripped over Mercutio and fell headlong into the orchestra pit.

Oh, I was wrong about the three-star reviews. No one gave us more than one.

23

Hannah's Gone

Andrew thinks I'm being a fool. He can't understand why I keep bursting into tears, says he's sick of seeing me with a face as long as a fiddle. I said, 'You don't have to look at me, Andrew,' and he went slamming out of the house. Really, at the moment, I hate my husband's guts, because, yes, he might be Hannah's father, but he's not her mother, and anyway he's a congenital idiot and he doesn't understand how it feels to have your heart ripped out. Seriously, the last time I ached this badly I had bronchial pneumonia and ended up in hospital on a nebuliser – but it wasn't as bad as this.

I can't eat. I feel sick, and I look out of the window and I see other mothers with their little girls, walking them to the primary school up the road. I see plaits bouncing and gym bags and scooters, and the tears just roll off my face. It's like I'm permanently peeling an onion; I just can't stop bloody crying, which is why I'm up here in Hannah's bedroom burying my face in her old dressing gown, the pink fleecy one that still smells of her, of strawberry shampoo and biscuits. I feel the black hole inside me open up again and I just want to climb into her bed and make the world disappear, because Hannah's gone and I can't bear it.

Andrew says I need to buck up. He says it's time she went: she's twenty-six, she needs to get on with her own life. We can't look after her forever, it's not healthy – but what he seems to forget is that Hannah's special. She needs extra care, always has, ever since she was born six weeks premature. Not that I remember much about it. Apparently I nearly died, lost almost every drop of blood in my body, but as soon as I regained consciousness they wheeled me down to special care. She was in an incubator, a tiny purple-skinned rabbit in a plastic fish tank. Three weeks before I could bring her home, then I carried her like she was made of meringue.

Most kids leave home at eighteen, says Andrew. Just because he did. Andrew's mother had four boys but I don't think she's very maternal. She's got one, lives in Shanghai, she hasn't seen for three years. What kind of mother is that?

Hannah's promised to come home for Sunday lunch. She might even sleep over, back here, in this bed where she belongs. Just because she's moving in with her boyfriend, it doesn't mean she has to stay there every night.

I'll do her favourite, roast chicken. Only the white meat for Hannah, just the breast, she doesn't like bones.

She's always been a faddy eater. She was about eight before she ate a vegetable. I swear that child lived on Frosties. She's still a cereal girl: there's a bowl under her bed, see, a Peter Rabbit bowl. She got the whole set as a christening present from her godmother. There's only the eggcup and this bowl left. I'll have to give that a good soak, muesli caked on like cement, but just the sight of it reminds me of when she was really little and it sets me off again.

Andrew says Hannah doesn't know where the dishwasher is, or the washing machine or the tumble dryer. oh, hang on, there's another stripy bowl and a couple of mugs. I was wondering where that one had got to. Bit pongy, all mould and soggy fag ends.

I don't think Jonty smokes. He's a fitness instructor, so it's unlikely. 'That's a laugh,' says Andrew, 'Hannah hooking up with a fitness instructor. She's that bone idle she can barely walk to the bus stop.' I say, 'She wouldn't have to walk to the bus stop if you weren't so mean.'

Thing is, he bought her a car for her twenty-first, but she had an unfortunate incident a week later. Brand-new silver Seat Ibiza, wrapped it around a tree. It was her friend Nicole's fault: they were driving home from the pub and Nicole started mucking around with the stereo and Hannah got distracted. The next thing we knew, there was a phone call from the police.

I swear my heart stopped, didn't take a beat again until I knew she was all right. She must have a guardian angel watching over her – not a scratch. Nicole, on the other hand, broke her pelvis in three places. Tragedy really, but if she'd not been messing about with the dashboard it wouldn't have happened in the first place.

Anyway, the car was a write-off, and because the police were involved Hannah was breathalysed, which I thought was unfair considering it was done when she was very badly traumatised, and I'm sure the upset and the adrenalin affected the result. Well, it must do, mustn't it? If she'd been allowed to come home and have a nice rest and a cup of tea I'm convinced she wouldn't have been over the limit. As it was, she was only a tiny bit over, and she'd have been totally under if Nicole hadn't bought her a double vodka at last orders in the pub. Hannah swore on her grandmother's life she only asked for a small. I'm not blaming Nicole, not entirely. I saw her in town a few weeks back, poor girl's still got a terrible limp.

I pretended to be looking at shoes in the window of Russell & Bromley. Which reminds me: I think Hannah might have taken my tan suede ankle boots, though they might have accidentally gone into one of those bin liners in the corner.

She promised she'd take the bags down to the charity shop. She must have forgotten, what with the excitement of moving.

It's a bit poky, the flat. We went to see it: partially furnished, hideous sofa, made Hannah cry it was so ugly. She begged her daddy to buy them a new one as a moving-in present, and there are some very good sales on leather sofas at the moment, but Andrew said no, so I crocheted her a throw. All bright colours, something she can curl up in when Jonty is out doing his personal training.

It's been two weeks since she went. I just wish he'd make it official, I wish he'd just get down on one knee. It's not like he can't – I've seen him doing his lunges. There's nothing wrong with his knees. It's the least he could do after what Hannah's been through over the past couple of years. Being bullied by her tutor at college, not being able to train as a hairdresser because touching old women's scalps made her feel physically sick, getting the job as a receptionist and accidentally falling in love with the boss, and who could blame her?

Grant was a very good-looking man. He used to drop her off in his Audi and I would say, 'Hannah, bring him in, we'd love to meet him. Tell him he's welcome any time.' Took her on a weekend to a boutique hotel in Exeter – his and hers massages, the lot – then his wife came round, caused a scene on the front lawn. Andrew had to go out and calm her down. Hannah was so upset she was running round the house tearing at her hair extensions. I tell you, I'm still finding them now, long peroxide extensions down the back of the sofa, acrylic fingernails in my Hoover.

She was pregnant, this woman, and well, hormones can make you very possessive. She had a foul mouth on her. I felt sorry for Grant, married to this screaming, shouting banshee. Anyway, it's all water under the bridge now. Only I don't think we realised what a toll it was taking on Andrew, because a week or so later he had a funny turn in the garden centre. Went dizzy and passed out, took down a stand of lobelia and a Roman centurion garden statue, although why anyone wants a six-foot Roman centurion in their garden is beyond me. Nearly killed him – not the heart attack, but the ruddy great statue!

A week in hospital and he was as right as rain. Double bypass; the doctor said he should take it easy in future, said stress was a likely contributing factor. I thought, Thanks, doc, don't talk to me about stress. I'm the one traipsing over to that hospital day in, day out.

Of course Hannah would have come with me, but she went off to Tenerife with some of her mates to get over Grant.

I said, 'Did you honestly not know he was married?' And

she just pulled this funny sort of idiot face, and I was relieved because I knew then she hadn't a clue. Poor little mite. No wonder she needed to get away from it all. I just wish she hadn't got that silly tattoo while she was on her holiday.

'That which does not kill you makes you stronger', all in fancy writing across the base of her neck. I tell you, if Jonty does ask her to marry him she can't go backless, not with an updo anyway.

I'll just have a quick peek in a couple of those bin liners and see if I can find my boots. I'm not sure which bags are for the bin, which are for the charity shop. I make sure everything goes to the British Heart Foundation, ever since Andrew's op.

Let's start with this bag here, it needs re-bagging anyway: ruddy great rip in it. Well, I've never seen this before: cashmere, funny colour – a cross between baby sick and mustard. It probably looked different in the shop. She's always been dressy, even as a little girl. If she got a speck of dirt on something she'd have to get changed. She liked everything new, which is why she got into such a mess with her online shopping: parcels from ASOS every other day. In the end we forced her to admit how much debt she'd got herself into. Two and a half grand overdrawn: that's why her father still has to pay for her mobile phone. She can't get a contract under her own name – failed the credit checks.

But this is definitely rubbish – all her old college files. After the hairdressing she was going to do hospitality and tourism, but apparently it was very boring and, as Hannah said, she didn't want to be treated like a kid and given homework, and anyway, all her lectures were at nine o'clock in the morning and how could that be fair when loads of other people didn't start 'til gone eleven? I think some of these textbooks might belong to the college library. Broken hairdryer. I tell you, Hannah and her hair, it's a full-time job. At the moment she's got it dark chocolate with dip-dyed caramel ends. She went all the way to London, into the West End, to get it done properly, because, as she said, no one round here has a clue. She ended up with the same stylist that does some of the girls from *Made in Chelsea*. Andrew just laughed and said, 'I bet they all say that,' and Hannah was that mad she wouldn't eat her tea. He can be very insensitive sometimes.

Hannah's like me, gets upset very easily, and she can't wear anything that makes her skin itch. That's why she has to have cashmere . . . Lots of empty fake tan bottles in here, dried-up nail varnishes, a magnifying mirror with a dirty great crack across it, old bras – she's a fiend for new under-wear – and my boots, or rather one of my boots. Where's the other one?

Don't tell me you've lost it, Hannah. How can you lose one boot? Mind you, Hannah can lose anything, keys, purse, passport. Oh, here it is, the other boot. Well, no wonder she hid it: the bloody heel's come off. Cost me a fortune, these boots, and now they're all squashed and broken. She can be a bit careless, can Hannah, charging around, doing whatever she likes, leaving a trail of devastation and not even noticing the damage she's done. She doesn't think to think, that's her problem. Like not finding out if Grant was married, and then running away to Tenerife to get over him. Only she wasn't just getting over just him. I discovered the paperwork when she asked me to find her passport – see, that's how careless she is. A termination; Grant's baby, I suppose. I just kept quiet, handed over the passport, gave her the cab fare to the airport and didn't tell Andrew, because he was lying in hospital all stitched up looking like a shark had taken a chunk out of him. When Hannah came home I was so glad to have her safely back, because she'd only texted once in ten days, that I forgot to mind about the other thing. Only I did mind, but I couldn't say anything. I couldn't tell her that I knew, so I just let her see how upset I was about the tattoo. But she said it was *her* skin on *her* neck and I had to stop being such a hysterical bitch, and about a week later she started seeing Jonty and he's got tattoos all over. She's moved on, she's just left us behind with the rest of the crap she can't be bothered with any more, like the sofa throw I made her. That's in this bin liner too, shoved under a load of ancient *Grazia* magazines. I start crying again, and as I wipe my face on Hannah's old dressing gown I realise that actually it stinks of cigarettes and cheap perfume and too many late nights; there are big smears of foundation round the collar and lipstick stains on the sleeves. It's a great big stinking rag in need of a good wash, and that goes for the rest of this room, with its grubby pillowcases and curling-tong burns on the carpet.

The whole room needs fumigating, if you ask me. I need to strip the bed, get rid of these sickly pink walls, paint it white and put all this rubbish on a bonfire, because I'm not sorting it all out, it's too late. Hannah's gone, and once this room is redecorated and I've made up the bed with crisp new sheets and my lovely crocheted throw, it'll make a lovely spare room. In fact, I might even get a lodger.

A nice clean lodger, a young man maybe, with a proper job. Someone who keeps regular hours, doesn't smoke in bed and can help Andrew in the garden.

And I pull myself together and decide to make myself a nice cup of coffee, only halfway down the stairs I hear my mobile ring. Hannah's name comes up on the screen and for a second I dither, but then I think, no, she'll only want something, and right now I don't feel like talking to her.

And I put the kettle on instead.

24

Points

I don't usually borrow Brendan's car, it's too big. You need a ladder to climb into it, like driving a bin lorry. 'Bloody expensive bin lorry,' says Brendan. It's a BMW X7, which Brendan says is like a Range Rover but better.

All I know is it's black and it reminds me of when I went pony riding when I was little, and one day they ran out of ponies and they put me on a big stampy black horse. Terrified the living daylights out of me.

Bloody thing, I can never remember where the ignition is. Ah, here we go: dashboard lights up like Blackpool illuminations. It's very high-tech. Good, I don't need to stop for petrol. OK, let's get this postcode into the satnav. Where are my glasses? On top of your head, Gail!

I'm heading for a boutique in Corbridge, Damsels in dis

Dress. Silly name. I'd not heard of it, but apparently Gina Gleeson swears by it and she's never out of *Country Life*.

He doesn't surprise me often, Brendan, and it was a lovely thought, but it's been a while since I've been a size twelve. I'm a solid fourteen and I like a sleeve because I've gone a bit crêpey around the upper arm. Brendan says I should take up a racquet sport, just because he plays squash ... Here we go: NE45 6NH.

I usually drive a Figaro. 'Figaro?' says Brendan. 'Sounds more like a biscuit than a car,' but he still got me one, and at least it doesn't beep for no reason whatsoever.

Whoops! Handbrake, Gail. I never put mine on: you can't forget to take it off then, can you? Ha!

I'm better off in something small and nippy because coming off the bend and into our drive can be a bit tricky. You have to come in at just the right angle or smack, you've hit one of the pillars.

Brendan's put lions on top of them. He likes to play lord of the manor – that's why he got this beast of a car, so he can play hunting and shooting with his mates. He's got all the kit, I swear. Look: deerstalker on the passenger seat! I'd chuck it out the window, but he'd only get another.

Here come the pillars: the warning sensors are going mad. I've no idea how to shut them up. Breathe in, don't panic, Mrs Mainwaring, and we're through.

Whoops, didn't mean to do that. Apparently it's rude to toot. Ha!

I hope they've got something more suitable in this Damsels place. I don't know what Brendan was thinking; I've got good legs but I can't do above the knee. We've got Geoff and Tina's silver wedding anniversary lunch next week. Tina's in a state about the food. I said just get the caterers in, that's what I did for Brendan's fiftieth. We had a *Downton* theme, asparagus feuilletés, Calvados-glazed duck, parmentier potatoes. They even offered me a kidney soufflé, which was apparently a big hit on the *Titanic*, but in my opinion there's a fine line between authentic and disgusting.

I hired three maids and a butler, and we all dressed up. Thousands of sequins, all shimmering in the candlelight. Brendan and I had been taking private Charleston lessons for weeks.

Table Angels – Heavenly Dining: they do all sorts. I was going to go Hawaiian, but Brendan's birthday is in February and anyway, I once wore a coconut-shell bra for an am-dram *South Pacific*, and talk about chafing. Never again, so we went full-on *Upstairs, Downstairs*. One of Brendan's mates came as a drag Mrs Patmore. Brendan loved it, said it was the best present ever. He's been in a good mood ever since, and there was me thinking turning fifty would make him sulky.

I wish he wouldn't smoke in the car, it's disgusting. Always a tin of cigarillos in the glove box. 'My car, my rules,' says Brendan. 'My house, my rules. Work hard, play hard.'

He's a very competitive man, won't let anyone beat him at anything, not even his own son. I say give him a break, he's only fifteen. The kids are at boarding school. Louis and Gemma – she's just turned thirteen. Fees are astronomical, but Brendan says it's an investment. Like my boobs: he bought me a new set a couple of years ago because, as he said, they'd gone like flat tyres and needed pumping up.

I went for silicone rather than saline. There's quite a few of us round here who've been to the same man. 'Best of the breast', Brendan calls him, and he might be very good but he went in too deep, cut some muscle and I can't drive a non-automatic any more. There's scar tissue under the left armpit, so basically that side doesn't work like it used to, but as Brendan reminded me, 'You're right-handed, so what's the big deal?' And anyway, as he says, 'No one in their right mind drives a manual.'

Let's see if I can find the radio. Honestly, I feel like Sandra Bullock in *Gravity* – if I press enough buttons I might get Radio 2.

Oh hell's bells, that's the heating. I don't need that: I'm a woman of a certain age. Now, where's it gone?

I press a few more random buttons and then this voice comes out of nowhere. I swear I could have jumped through the sun roof. *Take the next exit on the left.*

Dear God, I've only gone and put the satnav on speaker mode. I didn't know who that was for a second. Whoops! Get a grip, woman. That's the windscreen wipers, you silly moo, indicator must be on the other side. I don't want the voice thingy, I was happy with just the map. How do I get it back to where it was? No, I don't want it on 3D. How do I get rid of—

Straight ahead for nought point five miles.

Oh sod it, I'll just do what I'm told. That's what Brendan says: 'Just do what you're told for once.'

Take the second exit after the roundabout.

Yes, miss. When I first met Brendan, and he'd had a few drinks, he used to sound like an old episode of *Only Fools and Horses*. He's probably installed a posh-sounding satnav just to keep his vowel sounds on the straight and narrow, a kind of in-car elocution lesson.

Drive straight ahead for three point two miles.

Don't mind if I do. I might get some new shoes too. I

always shop when I'm bored, and I've been bored ever since I finished decorating my garden office.

'What do you need a garden office for?' says Brendan. 'You don't work.' But we both know that's not the point and anyway, maybe I'd like a business, just a little sideline, like Table Angels. Or a little shop, you know the kind of place, that sells candles and bath oil. I'm smelly candle-mad, me. Sometimes I just sit in my office, lighting and blowing out candles. Which reminds me: I'm fifty this year. I'd like a little dog, but Brendan won't let me, so I might get a tummy tuck, or a hot tub.

Take the second turning on the left.

This must be a cut-through. I think Brendan's satnav makes its own mind up which way to take you. Apparently it's got a doo-dah that detects hold-ups. I'm probably avoiding some roadworks.

It's not very nice around here and I know it's silly, locking myself in, but you never know. A friend of mine was coming home from seeing *The Vagina Monologues* at the Theatre Royal, stopped at some lights and two lads got in and took the rings off her fingers. She was so shocked that when the lights changed to green she just drove home. Shock makes you do funny things. She said she was on autopilot 'til it hit her next day, and then she said she was so angry she'd have cut their hands off with a bread knife.

I've got a diamond solitaire engagement ring and an eternity ring – sapphires and diamonds – which Brendan bought me when Louis was born. He said the sapphires were the blue of the baby's eyes; he can be very romantic, can Brendan. I didn't like to tell him all babies have blue eyes. Louis's were brown by the time he was six months old. Still, it's a nice ring and it's worth a few bob.

I got a watch for Gemma. Cartier, mind.

Take the second turning on the right.

I don't think I've ever been up here. Bit bleak, lots of funny little grey council houses, scrappy shops, mini-supermarkets selling scratch cards and horrible pink sausages, ugly dogs shitting on the grass verges. It's not in our catchment area. Brendan's in bespoke conservatories. It was my father's business: Brendan came to work for him, married the boss's daughter. My mother never liked him. She's got Alzheimer's now, so she's none the wiser: I could be married to Desmond Tutu for all she knows. Lives in a home, every day the nurses bring her down into the conservatory that my dad designed back in the eighties, and my husband helped to build – life's full of coincidences. I think my dad saw something of himself in Brendan. He was a self-made man, came from nothing. Gave him a leg-up, son he never had and all that.

In two hundred yards take the next turning on the left.

Here we go. You can heat this steering wheel if you like, and the seats, but they get too hot and it feels like I've wet myself.

You have reached your destination.

Well no, I've not, but I switch the ignition off anyway. This isn't Corbridge, this is a council estate in the arse end of nowhere. There's no artisan bread shop or exclusive ladies' fashion emporium round here.

Bloody satnav, tells you everything apart from what the

hell I'm doing here. I must have hit the wrong button when I was trying to find the radio. Where's me glasses? Says 14 Benfield Close. I've gone and pressed Recent History, that's what I've done.

Bit of a dump, if you ask me: wet sand-coloured pebble-dash, kids' plastic toys in the front garden, one of those little slides they grow out of in no time. Brendan got an architect to design an adventure playground in the back garden: tree house, rope swing, the lot. Sometimes when he's home from boarding school and Gemma's playing at a friend's house, my son sits in his tree house and smokes dope and I sit in my garden office and we both look out onto the back of our big house that hasn't got anyone in it.

I don't know what I'm doing sat here like cheese at four-pence. I'm going home. I switch the beast back on and out of habit I mutter, 'Mirror, signal, manoeuvre.'

Only I can't manoeuvre, because there's a bright pink van coming in the opposite direction and it pulls across the road and parks right behind me. Black loopy writing all over it: Table Angels, Food fit for the Gods. They've a logo of an angel flying out of frying pan, and even though it's rude to toot the van beeps its horn three times.

Almost immediately the door of number 14 opens, and I don't know why I'm relieved but I am. She's just a lumpy middle-aged woman in a porridge-coloured cardi. A Jack Russell runs out into the garden and has a sniff about. I don't want one of them, I want something soft and furry that I can carry under my good arm, like a chihuahua. She's holding a kid, a boy, a wriggly toddler, arching his back and screaming, and then a girl comes flying out, kisses the little lad on the head and runs down the path. It's one of the maids from Brendan's birthday party, one of my below-stairs. About twenty-three, size twelve, nice legs. I can't remember her name – why would I? She was in my house to take coats and serve drinks. She stops in her tracks on the pavement, stares at the car, looks straight at me and I look straight back. She blushes and I don't – why should I? She jumps in the pink van and shouts, 'Bye, Mum. Thanks, see you later,' and before I know it they've gone, but not before I noticed that her arms are very toned. Must be carrying all those big silver trays.

I drive very sensibly and carefully back through this crummy estate of crappy little houses. I'm breathing quite normally and I'm a bit too calm – my blood feels like a chilled Chablis in my veins – but gradually it gets warmer, and by the time I reach the dual carriageway it's scalding. My heart is a spitting furnace and I open the windows to get some air in. I need to feel the cold wind on my face, so I go a little faster.

Speed camera ahead.

Thanks for the tip. I pull my collar up, grab Brendan's stupid deerstalker, ram it on my head and put my foot down. He'll dispute it, swear blind it wasn't him, but there will be photographic evidence and anyway, what other idiot would do seventy in a fifty-mile-an-hour zone, wearing a deerstalker hat in black BMW X7?

Poor Brendan, I'm the only one who knows he's in bed with a temperature of 101, and even though I spent three grand on hypnotherapy to quit smoking, I light a cigarillo, and as the speed camera flashes I am smiling for the birdie.

I must be doing seventy in a fifty-mile-an-hour zone when I have one last stab at the dashboard for the radio and bingo, Brendan's special-edition speakers vibrate as Meat Loaf yells 'Like a bat out of hell . . . ' which is apt, if not my cup of tea.

Obviously, I am back in the village in record time. I jump a red light on my approach; a cyclist shouts but I just laugh and throw the smouldering cigarillo at his helmeted head. I see him write the registration number on the back of his hand, before I undertake a bus and enter one of those boxes you're not meant to enter unless your exit is clear, which it isn't.

My blood is pumping now and I take a sneaky illegal right-hand turn into the supermarket car park and nip the wrong way down a one-way street onto the road up to our house. Now, normally I am very careful on the approach to our driveway. As I've said, it's a very tricky corner, but today I don't care. This car is like a tank, and right at the last moment, just before I miss the entrance completely, I pull down hard left on the wheel, only what with my scar tissue, I don't have the strength – sorry, Brendan. There is a ghastly scraping sound of metal against brick and an accompanying scream of outrage from the sensors.

Whoops-a-daisy, that'll be two cars in the garage now, not that Brendan will be needing his for a while. He's already got nine points on his licence; add those to the ones I've collected for him today and he's well over his limit. Poor Brendan, if he wants to visit his little girlfriend in the future he'll have to catch a bus.